SHELTERED BY THE SEAL

A *H.E.R.O. FORCE* NOVEL

SHELTERED
BY THE SEAL

AMY GAMET

USA TODAY BESTSELLING AUTHOR

Layton, Felder, Bach & Moore
Attorneys-at-Law
58 East 42ndStreet, Suite 1800
New York, New York 10016

Maria Elena Cortez
167 Lake Avenue
Savannah, Georgia 31407

Dear Ms. Cortez,

I am acting as the executor of the estate of Mr. Harold Hopewell, whose Last Will and Testament was entered into probate in the Surrogate's Court, New York County, State of New York.

I write to inform you of certain assets bequeathed to you pursuant to Mr. Hopewell's Last Will and Testament, to wit: a first edition copy of *The Manor* by John Boronkay.

Please do not hesitate to contact me with any questions.

Regards,
Frederick Bach, Esquire

CHAPTER 1

"YOU HAVE MY sincerest condolences, Peter. Your uncle was a very good man."

Peter Hopewell slipped his hands into the silk-lined pockets of his trousers and looked out at New York City through the rain-flecked glass. "Thank you, Fred." He turned to the lawyer. "What happens now?"

"We at Layton, Felder, Bach & Moore will handle the distribution of the inheritance per Mr. Hopewell's instructions."

"What does that mean, exactly?"

"We'll mail the bequeathed items directly to the heirs, along with a letter explaining they are being willed to them from your uncle. If for some reason a letter is returned as undeliverable, we'll attempt to locate the heir. If we're unable to find him or her, the unclaimed inheritance will pass to you along with the rest of the estate."

Peter nodded and walked to a table full of items, his fingers running over the aged leather cover of a small red book. "Very well." He opened the cover, his eyes falling on the familiar words.

"I wonder if she'll realize what she has," said Peter.

Fred laughed. "Knowing your uncle, he'd probably rather she just enjoy the story than know its value."

Peter laughed, too. "That's exactly right." He closed the book and gritted his teeth. "Stupid old man. More money than God, and he had no idea what to do with it."

The other man's eyes widened, the only indication he'd heard the words at all.

"Well then, I guess there's nothing left to be done." Peter held out his hand.

The lawyer shook it. "I'll be in touch if we are unable to locate any of the heirs."

"Sounds good." Peter moved to take his hand away, but Fred held it.

"I am glad you decided not to contest your uncle's will," said the lawyer. "Harold was of sound mind, and these are his wishes."

"Yes. Controlling everyone from beyond the grave, just as he did in life."

Or trying to.

Peter walked out of the lawyer's office and into the rain as a plan came sharply into focus. His uncle was dead. He was in charge now.

CHAPTER 2

JAX ANDERSSON RAN his finger around the top of his old-fashioned glass of whiskey, ignoring the raucous laughter of a group down the bar and letting the world slip out of focus.

He'd seen enough for today.

"Another?" asked the bartender, and Jax nodded once. He sat up straighter and tossed the rest of his drink back, pushing the glass toward the bartender.

"You visiting someone in town?" he asked Jax.

An image flashed in his mind, Jessa's tortured face as she reached to slam the door behind him, and his stomach heaved. "No." He picked up his drink and turned his attention to the TV, letting his eyes close too long between blinks. The whiskey was doing its magic.

The bartender began wiping the bar but stopped and turned his head when the bell over the door jingled. "Evening. How're you doing tonight?" he asked.

"Good, thank you."

Jessa.

Jax couldn't have helped the whip of his neck if he'd tried. There she was, standing in front of the door, coolly assessing his stare, and his balls clenched tightly.

God, she's gorgeous.

Long black hair to her waist, straight as an arrow. Wide-set eyes so brown they were nearly black. Amber skin that seemed to glow from within, her Cherokee heritage shining through time. He could have drawn her picture, he'd imagined her face so often.

She slowly began moving toward the bar. To the bartender, she said, "I'll take a glass of Cabernet, please." She sat down beside Jax and turned to him with a polite smile. "Hi, Jax."

Her arm was brushing his, the lightest touch setting his skin on fire. The alcohol that had been a blessing just moments before was now an eraser, firmly rubbing out the line between how he should treat the widow of his friend and his pronounced attraction to this woman. His eyes were homing in on hers in an animalistic way that screamed, *I want you.*

He ripped his gaze away and sucked in a deep breath. He didn't want to be around her right now, hadn't planned on any company. He'd been wound tight when he checked in at the hotel across the street and come here hours earlier after leaving her house, and he would have sworn the whiskey had long since made him numb.

Except that numbness was being replaced by something else far more dangerous—an urgent need for sensation.

"Hey," he said, searching her face for some kind of explanation. Hours before, she'd slammed the door in his face and sent him away after he'd driven all night to tell her the news he'd waited years to deliver.

We killed the man who murdered your husband.

It should have given her closure. Relief. Happiness. But instead she'd gotten angry.

So angry.

What had possessed her to come looking for him? He spoke deliberately, wanting to sound more sober than he was. "Didn't think I'd be seeing you again so soon."

The bartender brought her wine and she fiddled with the stem. "I calmed down."

His eyes roamed over her face, as tangible as a touch. Just to look at this woman gave him more pleasure than almost anything he could do with another, the closeness of her body beside him warming him like the heat from a fire.

She sighed. "I knew I owed you an apology for the way I acted earlier. I didn't want that to be the last thing I ever said to you."

The finality of her words made his jaw clench. While it had been two years since he'd last seen her face, she'd been in his life on some level or another for far longer than that, and he wasn't prepared to let her go.

What do you expect, now that Ralph's dead?

When her husband was alive, he and Ralph worked together on HERO Force, the Hands-on Engagement and Recognizance Operations team. The group of former Navy SEALs and alphabet agency frontmen was a tight-knit group, and as Ralph's wife, Jessa had held a place in it from the beginning.

Long enough for Jax to know her well and realize what a lucky bastard Ralph was to have her. Hell, maybe he was even a little jealous.

Then Ralph was gone, and Jax was left with a desire for Jessa he had no right to act upon. Sitting next to her right then, the smell of her perfume light on the thick barroom air, he was covered in her, steeped in her presence and beginning to drown.

Who would have thought he had it in him?

He wasn't sober enough to have an appropriate conversation with Jessa. He wasn't drunk enough, either, because her stare was making its way down his chest and back up to his eyes, and he didn't know what to do with that beyond throwing her on the bar and showing her what that stare was doing to him.

He took a sip of his whiskey, the alcohol burning its

way down his throat with a welcome flame.

She put her hand on his forearm. "Say something, Jax. You're always so quiet."

Pleasure shot through him at the contact. His eyes dipped to her neck and the straps of her small silver tank top glistening in the dim light of the bar. She was dripping in sex appeal. Soaked in it as if she'd deliberately bathed in its waters tonight.

A thousand comments came to mind, not one of them casual enough to cross his lips. His voice was hoarse. "What do you want me to say?"

"Tell me how things are going. We haven't talked in so long."

"HERO Force?"

Pain flashed in her eyes. "No. You."

I am HERO Force.

He reached for his drink. What else was there? He'd started HERO Force. Lived it every day, showered with it, lifted weights and fired guns with it. He'd hand selected the others and chosen the jobs they took on. If HERO Force was off-limits as a conversation topic, he was damn near out of options beyond *I want to see you naked.* He slipped into his comfortable mask of nonchalance and shrugged. "I'm good."

He shifted in his seat. He was already sporting wood from sitting so close to her, his mind running free of its reins from the alcohol he'd consumed. This was Jessa his arm was brushing up against, Jessa who was staring so intently at him, Jessa who was like a siren screaming for his attention.

And she had it. She'd always had it.

"Are you seeing anyone?" she asked.

He nearly spit out his whiskey and wiped his lips with the back of his hand. "No."

She smirked and bumped against him. "You don't take women out to dinner and a movie? Invite them to spend the night?"

The physical contact and the intimacy of the question made adrenaline burst into his bloodstream. "Sure."

"Well, that's seeing someone." She grinned.

He stared into her eyes, needing her to understand.

Her smile fell.

"I don't see them at all," he said. It was the closest he'd come to crossing the line, as close as he'd allow himself to go without an invitation. He watched her reaction intently, like a poker player searching for a tell.

She took a sip of her drink, the glass trembling in her hand. Her face flushed, the high color making her amber skin glow.

"Let's talk about you," he said. "Are you seeing anyone?"

"No."

"No dinners, no movies, no sleepovers?" He might have been copying her question, but his tone of voice was dripping with every implication he wanted to voice.

She lifted her head and stared at the bar, her rib cage rising and falling with each breath. "No."

Jesus, she hasn't been with anyone since Ralph.

Blood rushed to his cock. He shifted on his barstool. It was too much, all of it. This woman. Her outfit. The little touches and bumps of her body into his. And she hadn't had sex with anyone *in years.*

She must be starving for the connection sex could bring, the physical release. She'd been grieving her husband, of course. But a woman like that would have every opportunity for love, and she'd taken none of them.

She's a mother. She's busy, not sitting around wishing for a man.

"The baby must take up a lot of your time," he said, wondering again if she'd had a boy or a girl. He opened his mouth to ask, but she held up her hand.

"I don't want to talk about the baby. I came here to get away from all that."

"Did you?"

"Yes."

"Why else did you come here, Jessa?"

The air between them was thick. His hand clenched his glass on the bar, and he forced his grip to relax before it shattered. She looked nervous now. Her eyes dropped to her wineglass and she was clearly considering her answer.

"I was tired of packing," she said. "A little sad thinking about leaving the place I've lived for years. I figured a drink would be nice."

That was a lie. He'd been trained to tell. She'd been packing, all right, but something else had sent her in search of him, and he wanted—needed—to know what it was.

"You knew I would be here," he said.

Her fingers tightened on her wineglass. "I'm lonely, Jax."

Fuck.

He felt like he'd been sucker-punched, her words like some sort of attack on his restraint.

She turned toward him fully, resting her hand on his forearm again, the sensation traveling up his arm and down lower, lighting up his senses.

"It's been so hard," she said. "I've been by myself for so long, and then today you were there and…I thought maybe…"

The pulse in his groin was throbbing now.

She licked her lips. "Maybe we could be together."

Be together?

She wanted to spend the night with him.

No. He must have misunderstood. She was looking for conversation, a friend to catch up on old times with, nothing more, and he worked to reign in his enthusiasm. She stared at him, waiting for a reaction, but he had no idea what to say.

She blew out air and pushed her wine away. "I made a mistake. I shouldn't have come." She stood up and his hand shot out, grabbing her forearm tightly.

"Wait." Beneath his grip, she was warm and soft and too much of what he wanted. He held on tightly, his thumb stroking her tentatively. "I just want to make sure we're on the same page."

She pulled her arm away. "Never mind."

"Jessa, if you're saying you need someone to talk to, I'll be here for you. And if you need a shoulder to cry on, you're always welcome to use mine."

She didn't look up.

"But that's not what you're asking me for, is it?"

She squeezed her eyes shut, and he touched her chin to tip her face up. "Open your eyes."

A beat passed before she complied, her eyes open to his, the truth shining in their glassy depths. She was asking him to make love to her.

He took a quick breath in. "Let's get out of here."

CHAPTER 3

J ESSA WALKED DOWN the hotel hallway with Jax, the smell of whiskey trailing behind him like exhaust. She felt disconnected from her body, as if it were someone else who'd asked him to take her here, someone else who was going to have sex with him and hold his seed inside her tightly with a wish and a prayer.

Please let me get pregnant tonight.

She couldn't believe she was going through with this.

She'd been so angry when he showed up at her safe little house this morning and threw the most horrible event of her past on the floor like a hunter dropping a bloody carcass. And he thought she'd be happy! After all this time, he finally killed the bastard who'd murdered Ralph, as if that scum of the earth hadn't deserved to die long before her beloved husband.

So she'd slammed the door after he left and sunk to the floor, a puddle of emotion and grief. Hugging herself, she thought of how much that man had taken from her. The love of her sweet Ralph. The joy she'd always experienced in her husband's presence. She didn't smile anymore, didn't laugh—not the way she did then.

Worst of all, he'd taken away her child, her identity as a pregnant woman waiting with a happy heart to become a mother.

He'd taken away love. He'd left only darkness.

Her skin grew chilled as time passed, the room getting darker. Then an idea appeared in her mind like a single, welcoming light after a cold, dark night.

Jax can give me a baby.

It was horrible, really, for even in that moment she had no intention of allowing him to be a father. And while she never would have condoned keeping a baby's paternity a secret, she had no moral qualms about keeping a baby from Jax Andersson.

He owed her two people. She'd only be taking back one.

But you'll have to sleep with him.

Since Ralph, the idea of sex with anyone else held no appeal. Where she'd once been a very sensual being, now she was dead inside, all dried up like mud in a desert.

It would be hard enough to have sex, but with Jax? She had so much anger tied up in her head with that man, would she even be able to do it?

It's not like I'll enjoy it.

He was an odd man, mechanical and emotionally stiff. She'd heard him called the Tin Man, and laughed because the description was so perfectly coined. He was hardly one to inspire feeling or emotion, which was perfect, as she surely didn't want either one.

But oh, how she wanted to be a mother.

Jax opened the hotel room door, the sound of the deadbolt sliding home slamming her back to the present. She was standing in the overly bright hallway, about to sleep with a man she hated.

Fear had her taking a step back, but Jax guided her in front of him with his hand on her back. She fought the urge to wriggle away from his touch.

You want a baby, don't you? And who better to give you one than the man who killed the last one?

She felt a visceral ache in her lower abdomen as she did whenever she thought of her miscarriage, coming just a day and a half after she learned of Ralph's death. There was no doubt in her mind it was her grief that had ended her baby's life, sending her precious little boy straight to heaven to be with his father, and bypassing Jessa entirely.

It was Jax who sent Ralph on that mission. Jax who had the intel that told him it wasn't safe, Jax who stayed behind while her husband paid the price for the other man's bad decision.

The room smelled stale and the air conditioner was blasting cold air. She felt exposed in her spaghetti-strap top.

Not as exposed as you're about to be.

She began to panic. She wished she could sit down.

He turned to her, and she could feel the heat coming off him, the electric heat that threatened to overtake her. Even in the dim light he was so much larger than she was, his body taller and wider at the shoulders, his quiet, hulking personality hiding a strength she'd always found intimidating.

Plus the man didn't talk. It was painful to get him to engage in any kind of conversation, so she'd worried over how she was going to get him up here.

She needn't have bothered.

He took a step toward her and she jumped a little, the cold and her nerves jangling up inside her. Then his massive hands were on her upper arms, nearly reaching all the way around to meet at the other side, warmer than she wanted them to be.

She was standing ramrod straight, fear holding her still. This was Jax, the man who'd been the sole focus of her hatred for two solid years, and she was going to have sex with him? What the hell she been thinking? She shimmied her shoulders, wiggling away from his hands, and he let her go.

"This was a bad idea," she said. Tears were beginning to collect in the backs of her eyes, and she made a conscious effort to keep them there. "I don't know what I was thinking coming here."

She thought of the child she so wanted to carry. *I'm sorry, baby. I can't do this, not even for you.*

"It's okay."

She shook her head. "No, it's not okay." Maybe she should have had more alcohol. She hadn't even finished one glass. She walked backwards toward the door.

"You blame me for Ralph's death."

"I don't want to talk about that."

He walked toward her. "You blame me for his death, and you can't be with me because you think you'd be betraying your husband."

"I need to go."

"But you can feel how much I want you, how desperate I am to touch you, and you need to be wanted like that again, touched by hands that long to stroke your skin, feel the weight of a man on top of you, holding you down."

Her chin came up slowly, his words resonating inside her, vibrating down into her secret places and making her come alive. She did want those things. She needed to feel like a desirable woman, needed to be with a man.

But this man?

"You need to feel like a woman again, even if it's just for one night." He closed the distance between them. "I can do that for you, Jessa. I want to do that for you." He took her hand, the thick, strong fingers welcoming and warm.

Human touch.

It had been so long.

Her eyes drifted closed. The sensation of connecting with him like this in the dark was dizzying, terrifying. He trailed his other hand up her other arm, his nails skimming her flesh, and she took a small step toward him, her eyes still closed. Her head lifted as if on a string.

He kissed her, his lips light and gossamer on her mouth. The scent of alcohol was dangerous and new, and she opened her mouth to taste him. His hand clenched her upper arm and she felt the strength in his grip. A steady beat began to pulse between her legs, her jeans tight against her there as she began to swell with desire.

You can't enjoy this. This isn't about sex, it's about revenge.

But he deepened their kiss, forcing her to open herself to him more, commanding her mouth to give and receive pleasure, and she hovered on the brink of fighting him or giving in.

Her chance to change her mind was quickly passing her by. Her skin was hot and her traitorous body was desperate for this connection, egging her on and ramping up her desire even as her mind worked to tamp it back down.

Her eyes popped open as Jax kissed down her neck, the smallest cry escaping from deep in her chest as he sucked lightly on her skin. She pushed his body away.

"It's okay to enjoy another man's body, Jessa."

No, it's not.

She wanted to cry. She couldn't do this. Couldn't contain the experience in some little box forged of hatred and steel. Sex was too personal, too important to her, and she'd forgotten how damn good it could feel. She couldn't let Jax be the one to bring passion back into her life.

"I shouldn't have come here."

"Because you don't want to be here, or because you do?"

He walked backwards, his eyes never leaving hers as he pulled her toward the bed, then sat down on its edge and pulled her onto his lap.

His hands rubbed her legs, her hips, and held her tightly against him as he kissed her, his mouth demanding a response.

When she hesitated, he pulled the covers back and dragged her beneath them. He wrapped his arms around her middle and pulled her tightly against him with a growl, his erection pressing into her upper abdomen. It felt good, so good to be wanted like this, but she held back, unable to respond to him any more than she already had.

Then something changed.

Jax slowed down.

His kisses were now focused on her skin instead of her mouth, his hands massaging and scraping and slipping against her overly sensitized body. Every touch was like an assault on her good judgment, making her long to respond to him even more, and he wasn't even touching her most intimate places.

God, if he did that, she would be lost…

His mouth moved back to hers, lightly kissing and cajoling her response, his tongue exploring and tasting.

"Kiss me, Jessa," he ground out against her mouth. "Kiss me and I'll take off your shirt and touch you there." She imagined his hands on her breasts, her nipples, his talented mouth lapping at her peaks. She wanted it so badly she was powerless to deny herself.

The slightest sob escaped her as she kissed him back, her tongue reaching into his mouth, and the kiss exploded with fiery passion. He fitted his body between her legs and ground against her swollen sex, making her moan with pleasure.

The sound of her response was brazen, making her freeze up. This wasn't what she'd bargained for and was quickly getting out of control. Jax's hands were slipping up under her slinky top and lifting it over her head, and she covered her breasts with her arms despite her longing for his touch.

Jax braced himself on his arms and looked down at her.

What did he see? Was it fear or desire?

"Do you want to stop?" he asked.

She forced her arms back down to her sides. "No."

"Are you nervous?"

"Yes."

"Roll over."

She shot him a questioning look, but he only helped to flip her over. He sat on top of her legs, just below her derriere, and began to stroke her back.

If his kisses and earlier touch had felt good, she was unprepared for the sensation of his hands on her back. It had been years since someone had touched her this way, years since she'd received physical pleasure from another human being, and she nearly purred out loud.

She could feel the hard ridge of his cock pressing against her bottom through their jeans, but he took his time with her neck and shoulders, the muscles that lined her spine and the hungry flesh spread out before him.

Her excitement was growing, no matter that she didn't want it to, and she pressed her hips into the mattress to keep from arching her back in blatant invitation.

But Jax had started a fire and she was powerless to control it. Every touch of his hands was its own temptation, the movements of her body totally bound to his orchestration.

When Jax reached around her and unbuttoned her jeans, she eagerly helped him pull them from her body, grateful her face was pressed against the mattress so he couldn't see the desire flushing her face and chest. She was squirming beneath him now, her body desperate for his and her legs spreading apart.

There was no denying her excitement, no way to prevent her pleasure, and she gave in to the sensation when Jax stroked her bottom and caught the strings of her thong, pulling it up and deeper into her crevice.

She cried out.

"You like that?" he asked.

"Yes."

He pressed his bare cock against her bottom. "You know how good it's going to feel when I'm inside you?"

His words made her pelvis curl toward her abdomen.

"Get on your knees," he commanded, and she did as she was told, her back arching so that her ass went high in the air, exposing herself to him, the thin fuchsia panties the only barrier between their bodies.

Jax squeezed her cheeks in his hands, kneading the thick flesh and whispering reverent praise. He traced the line between the folds of her sex with one skillful finger, lightly settling on the bud hidden between them.

She wanted him to fuck her and get it over with, not draw it out like this and make her beg for him. But begging she was as he deftly teased her clitoris while pressing himself against her most sensitive places.

"Please, Jax."

"Please, what?"

"I need you inside me."

He cursed under his breath. "Roll over."

If she didn't face him, she could keep some semblance of herself away from him. "No. I want you like this."

"I want to see you."

She was nearly there, the finish line in sight, so she did as he asked, surprised by the size and breadth of his glistening cock, standing at attention.

He was bigger than her husband—the only other man she'd been with—and she wondered if he would hurt her. She let her eyes take in the rest of his body, so different from Ralph's.

Where her husband's muscles had been defined and trim, Jax's were big and bulging. He bent over her, nuzzling her neck, and her eyes closed once more. Then he was moving lower, taking her breast in his hand and squeezing it to a point before taking the whole of her nipple and areola into his mouth and sucking.

It was worse than she'd feared, pleasure searing through her, white hot and bright. The sensation overwhelmed her and she thrust her hips into his chest, bucking against him there while he suckled her harder.

"Please, Jax. I'm ready."

Had she ever been loved like this? Aroused to the point where she was begging for penetration, desperate for sexual release?

He moved lower, settling himself between her legs, and she was panting hard and heavy, knowing what he was going to do before his mouth settled over her secret place and she began the climb to orgasm.

She didn't want him to do this. It wasn't necessary to get pregnant, and she wanted only to do what was necessary.

"I want you inside me when I come, Jax."

He growled as he climbed on top of her, then tested his weight against her smaller frame. The feel of him was so good she could have cried. How she missed this! He wasn't even inside of her yet, and she was emotionally swamped by the return of these sensations after so much time without them.

He pressed the head of his cock beside her opening, and for a moment she thought she wouldn't have to deceive him. The slightest movement and he'd be inside her.

"You're so wet for me." He groaned. He was pushing hard against her, teasing her, so close to her entrance. "I need to get a condom."

She tightened her legs around his waist. "It's okay."

He was panting with the exertion of holding back. "What do you mean?"

She feared all of her anxiety and hopeful planning had been for nothing. She was right in the middle of her cycle, all the signs of her fertility clearly visible yesterday and today, but she needed to have unprotected sex with this man.

A risky thing to do, especially for a man who didn't like to take chances.

She held her breath, then reached between them, guiding his cock into her body with her hand. He thrust inside her with one long push, and they gasped with pleasure as he filled her.

He pulled out and thrust into her again, his cock stretching and stroking her tender flesh, and her physical joy mixed with her hope for a child.

"Are you sure it's okay?" he ground out.

She dug her nails into his back. "Yes."

"Jesus." He was breathing hard, pumping into her with hard strokes, forcing himself deeper inside her. "Do you want me to pull out?"

"No."

Please no.

She swallowed her fear. "Come inside me, Jax. I want you to."

It was like she hit a secret booster button in a video game. He let loose with a loud growl, the force of his thrusts instantly putting her on course for an orgasm.

The noises Jax made changed dramatically, and she knew he was beyond holding back. He thrust into her again and again, and she held her breath as her climax overtook her. Jax called out, buried to the hilt inside her body, and she smiled into the darkness as he came.

It was only when the aftershocks had stopped rippling through her that she again noticed the rumbling of the hotel air conditioner, the bitterly cold air in the room, and the uncomfortable weight of Jax on top of her.

Lust dissipated, leaving self-hatred and shame in its wake. She'd accomplished what she'd set out to do, but she hadn't wanted to enjoy it.

Tears filled her eyes as she pushed Jax off of her, collected her clothing, and made her way to the bathroom, dressing without looking at herself in the mirror.

She knew what she would see there.

Bed-tossed hair, her face flushed from exertion and desire. Maybe a hickey to complete her humiliation. She was the worst kind of person, unable to focus on her hatred of the man when his touch felt so good. Letting him fuck her was necessary. Begging him to fuck her and experiencing the most powerful orgasm of her life was utter and complete betrayal.

She pushed out of the bathroom.

In the dim light from the window, she could see Jax sitting up in bed.

"Are you okay?" he asked.

"I'm leaving now." She walked toward the door.

"You don't have to go, Jessa. Stay with me."

"No thanks." She opened the door and left, without so much as a glance in his direction.

She was never going to see Jax Andersson again.

CHAPTER 4

THE BLADES OF the chopper roared mightily, their vibration seeming to beat in time to the rhythm of Jax's heart. It was three in the morning and they were hugging the landscape, quickly approaching their target.

He closed his eyes, mentally preparing for the extraction. He visualized the layout of the house, the terrain he anticipated from their landing site to the backyard and French doors, where they'd be entering the home. It wasn't a big house, but it was big enough to hold a hostage.

The husband's voice played in Jax's head.

You have to get her back. I don't know who I am without her.

The poor guy was clearly still in shock, though the sentiment resonated with Jax like some kind of spiritual truth. He'd been a goddamn mess since he slept with Jessa, worse even than during his divorce. It was as if with one night together, his entire idea of who he was as a person had been bent over backwards and folded in on itself.

He was a man who liked to be alone.

He reveled in it, for God's sake.

People were a business he didn't invest in. These guys here—Red, Cowboy, Logan, and Hawk—were closer to him than anyone else on the planet. Hell, even when he was married to Linda he was closer to HERO Force than he was to his own damn wife, and that was just fine with him. It was natural. He was a rough, cold bastard. Calculating.

What did he have in common with a woman?

But for a moment in time, Jessa had changed all that. From the second she walked into the bar to the instant she walked out of his room, he was with her. Really with her. Like he was one of two, instead of his own person barely tethered to the human race.

He knew he was a considerate lover, always making sure he did what was necessary to give his partner pleasure, but this time he did those things because he wanted to kiss every part of her flesh and taste every hidden fold of her body, wanted to heighten her experience because his own was innately intertwined with hers.

And it had shaken him to the core.

That kind of connection didn't just walk into a bar and ask you to sleep with it. That kind of connection was something you held on to tightly and defended at all costs.

The chopper dipped and dove. They were getting close now.

You have to get her back. I don't know who I am without her.

He could see the path through the woods to the door in his mind's eye, knew how this would go down up until the moment they actually entered the house. Then it was anybody's guess. Was there one person guarding the wife, or two, or more? Did they have weapons in hand? A clear route of escape?

The wife had been taken from her kitchen two days earlier, a cutting board with half-sliced bread left staling on the counter and a toddler left watching TV. Her husband was a big-time CEO of some Fortune 500 company, and he'd made one too many enemies with his recent revitalization plan.

Her captors had requested a ransom of five point six million dollars. Instead they were going to get their own private war.

The chopper landed and Jax filed out between Hawk and Cowboy, night-vision goggles in place and an AK-47 in each of their hands. They were on a mission to retrieve Mrs. Baldwin, but it was Jessa's face Jax imagined as they made their way to those French doors and silently slipped inside.

The faint beeping of an alarm system keypad could be heard in the distance, and Red went in search of the sound. If they could destroy the keypad before the thirty-second window passed, the alarm system probably wouldn't go off.

The crunch of plastic and metal could be heard coming from the kitchen, followed by a piercing alarm that screeched through the house, assaulting Jax's ears.

So much for the silent approach.

He took the stairs two at a time, Hawk and Cowboy right behind him. Shots rang out from the top of the stairway and Jax returned fire, the shadow of a man half-hidden in a doorway.

Jax wore Kevlar.

Cleary, the other guy did not. Blood splattered the wall behind his falling body.

Jax went quickly around him, knowing one of his men would disarm the tango and be sure he posed no threat. He held his weapon at the ready and cleared the first hallway in search of Mrs. Baldwin.

The incessant wail of the security alarm continued in the background as Jax cleared the first bedroom and moved on to the second.

This time, Hawk went first. He rounded the corner with his gun at the ready. A man stepped out from behind the bedroom door with a pistol, and Jax let off three rounds right into the man's skull.

Hawk nodded and Jax turned back down the hallway toward the master suite, the only bedroom remaining. He knew Red was behind him, his weapon trained behind them in case more tangos emerged.

Jax inched toward the room and lightly pushed in the door.

Their hostage was tied to the bed, fully dressed, and Jax felt a moment's relief that it appeared she hadn't been sexually assaulted. A look of utter panic was on Mrs. Baldwin's face as her gaze shifted from Jax to a corner of the room he couldn't see from the doorway.

A string of shots was fired in the room, one after the other, splintering the wood door between Jax and his attacker. He stepped back so he could see through the crack at the door's hinges and returned fire, landing a shot clear into the tango's head.

The man fell to the ground.

Cowboy ran into the room and untied Mrs. Baldwin, who was screaming. Jax could hear him trying to calm her down as he and Hawk cleared the closets and bathroom off the master bedroom.

She continued to scream.

"I'll take her. You go with Hawk and clear the house," said Jax.

Cowboy nodded.

Jax sat on the bed next to Mrs. Baldwin and saw blood seeping out of the man he'd shot, the spreading stain like red paint spilling onto a carpet. He stood and covered the man with a towel, then came back to Mrs. Baldwin, whose screams had transformed into sobs.

Safe now.

Rescue.

Husband waiting.

"All clear," said Cowboy in Jax's earpiece.

When Mrs. Baldwin was quiet, Jax held out his hand for her to stand up, but she didn't move, so he picked her up and carried her out of the house.

They made their way back to the chopper, closed the door, and were back in the sky in twenty-two and a half minutes.

The woman cuddled in Jax's lap, clinging to him like a koala bear. But it was Jessa he imagined as he stroked her back, Jessa he saw as they flew back to reality.

Hours later when he fell into bed, Jax would remember the Baldwins reunited, clutching each other as love and horror spilled out onto the floor around them like the kidnapper's blood onto the carpet.

That was the part Jax would never have.

The reunion.

He cursed violently, punched his pillow, and rolled over.

CHAPTER 5

J ESSA AWOKE WITH a start, her eyes wandering around the room and trying to make sense of where she was. It took her a minute to remember this was her home now, the large apartment in the second-story walk-up of an old Victorian house.

She looked down at her outfit. Scrubs.

Ugh.

She'd walked in the door from working second shift at Mercy and flopped down on the couch. Judging by the sunlight shining in the windows, she'd slept here all night, the second time in the past week she'd done so.

The first trimester of her last pregnancy, she was crazy sleepy, too. She laid her hand on her flat lower abdomen and joy filled her heart. Just a week ago, a home pregnancy test confirmed what she suspected. She was going to have a baby.

She thought of the nursery she and Ralph had decorated together between his trips with HERO Force. They'd known they were having a boy, and everything was done up in blue and green.

Maybe this time, I won't find out the sex.

Why? So you can protect yourself from loving this child in case something happens?

"I already love you more than anyone in the world," she whispered.

Today was Friday, her day off, and she desperately wanted to spend the whole thing in bed with some fuzzy slippers and a book. But as her stare slipped guiltily to the boxes stacked three and four high along the dining room wall, she knew what she'd be doing instead. She'd already been here almost a month, and those boxes weren't going to get any easier to unpack as she got further along.

Resigned to the task ahead, she walked into the kitchen, started some decaf brewing and checked her cell phone.

One new message.

She hit the speaker button and opened the fridge, grabbing the orange juice.

"Jessa, it's Jax."

She spun around so fast she dropped the juice to the floor, where it sprayed everywhere. She crouched down after it, trying to find the hole while her body responded viscerally to Jax's voice. An image of them making love flashed through her mind.

"I want to take you out to dinner sometime," he said. "I know you moved to Savannah, but if you'd like to get together, I don't mind the drive."

She found the leak and covered it with her finger, then closed her eyes tightly.

"I'd really like to see you again, Jess."

The message ended, and she could hear her pulse pounding in her ears. Four weeks and three days she'd been gone, and he found her. Hell, he probably knew where she was even before that and just didn't pick up the phone. She stood up and dumped the juice container in the sink. She looked at her arms and hands and clothes. "Aaagh!" she yelled, so frustrated she couldn't see straight.

She hadn't counted on this in her quickly laid plans to get pregnant. Right now it wasn't such a big deal, but what if he looked her up six months from now, or a year? If he found out he had a child, he'd want to be part of its life, and that was definitely not part of her plan.

But what could she do? With the technology at his disposal, he'd be able to find her anywhere she went. All he had to do was type her name into his damn computers, and there she'd be.

Forever.

It might even tell him when she had a dependent.

There had to be a way to stop him, a way to keep

her whereabouts from popping up on a screen just by typing in her name.

My name.

A horrible idea came to her mind.

She'd chosen Savannah because her extended family was here, both her mother's upper-middle-class contribution and her father's shadier side of the family tree. Since her parents passed away, she was desperate to forge some deeper kind of connections with her living relatives.

Now that would never happen. She had closer family she needed to protect.

Two of her cousins had served time, one for stealing cars and the other for forgery. She grabbed her cell phone with shaking fingers. If memory served her correctly, her cousin Ricky's crime had been making fake IDs and selling them on the Internet.

Before that, they'd been friends. Long before. When her father was alive and well and trying to make a difference in the lives of his sister's children, who always seemed a little too far gone to be pulled back to safety. Ricky had certainly acted like he remembered her when she ran into him at her uncle's birthday party recently.

She opened her contacts, scrolling for her cousin's name, praying he would trust her enough to help her. "Ricky, it's your cousin, Jessa McConnell."

He sounded pleased to hear from her, and she

exhaled a breath she didn't realize she'd been holding. "I'm in trouble, really bad trouble." She bit her lip to keep her emotions from erupting. "I'm hoping you can help me."

CHAPTER 6

J AX HATED THE office.

They usually had a few days between missions to get caught up on the bullshit that needed to be done at a desk, and this time, each hour felt longer than the last. He had nothing to do but check email and think about Jessa.

He had to let it go.

She obviously had.

He turned the news on a small TV in the corner of the room and leaned back in his chair, remembering.

He'd gone to her house the day after they spent the night together, only to find a for sale sign in the yard and her cell phone disconnected.

She'd claimed she'd been tired of packing, when really she'd been finished. He'd tried to take that as the message it was no doubt meant to be.

I've moved on.

So should you.

He'd made the mistake of using the HERO Force computers to find out where she was. A little town just outside of Savannah, where she probably planted flowers outside her door and found a nursing job at the local hospital.

Of course he'd gotten her number and had to call her again, his pulse hammering at the sound of her voice on her greeting. He'd left a message.

She disconnected that cell phone the very same day.

He was two for two, and he couldn't help but wonder why she'd gone to such lengths rather than tell him she wasn't interested.

Overnight, he'd gone from a solitary man who enjoyed more than his share of female company to a goddamn loser who was stalking a one-night stand.

He might have been okay if he could have gotten her out of his mind, but the night they'd shared together was like a recording his memory played over and over again whenever he didn't have one hundred percent of his brain occupied. Like when he was checking email. Or—*God forbid*—trying to sleep.

That was the worst—whiskey and longing forming some kind of vortex that sucked him inside and refused to let go. There was only Jessa, her body and their lovemaking, her laughter and the spark in her eyes that had first drawn him to her.

I want you to come inside me, Jax.

He could hear her voice, see her face as she said the words.

Cowboy walked into Jax's office and sat down. "Hey, chief."

Irritation was instantaneous. "You know how to knock, Leo?"

Cowboy stood up, walked back outside, and knocked.

"Go the fuck away," said Jax.

"That's why I didn't knock." Cowboy closed the door and sat down again. "You want to tell me what's going on with you, man?"

"Paperwork. Office bullshit."

"You seem a little...what's the word? Bastardly. Some of the guys think you've just become a total jackass, but I think there's more to it."

"Are we having a heart-to-heart?"

"Sort of, yeah."

"Get the hell out of my office."

"Is it Linda?"

The mention of his ex's name was like a shock collar on an errant dog. "Jesus, no."

"But it is a woman."

Jax scowled. "Don't you have anything better to do?"

Cowboy shrugged and smiled. "Not really."

"Go to the range and shoot something. We got some new assault rifles I want you fully trained on before we go wheels up again."

"Already on it, chief. Red thinks they're too heavy, but I got the kill shot down."

"Then go do something else."

"Who is she? That hot little secretary who hit on you in the diner? Or the chick who lives downstairs and always wants you to give her a ride?" Cowboy pumped his hips.

"We're done here."

Cowboy was quiet for a minute. "What else could it be? Ever since you killed Steele, you've been acting like an asshole."

"Go find something to do, Cowboy."

"Wait a second…"

Jax glared at him, then picked up his coffee cup and moved to leave the room. He got so far as to put his hand on the knob.

"Is it Jessa?" asked Cowboy.

Jax froze, his eyes focusing on the shiny metal of the door in front of him. He'd been so close to getting away from this conversation.

Not close enough.

"Jax, what happened when you went to her house to tell her about Steele?"

Jax walked back to his desk. There was no point in denying it. "What do you want, Leo?"

"Do you want to talk about it?"

"No."

Cowboy leaned back in his chair, holding on to the desk and balancing on the back two legs. "'Cause, you know, you don't talk damn near enough. You should share with your friends. Get it off your chest."

"Fuck you."

"And your vocabulary could use a little work. You seem to keep using the same words over and over…"

"I can't find her," said Jax. Why not tell Cowboy? What difference would it make? He tapped his pen on the desk and sighed. "She moved away and she's not showing up in the system."

Cowboy slammed his chair down and stood, moving behind Jax's desk. "Let me try. I'm good at this."

Jax stood reluctantly. "I know how to do it."

Cowboy was on the computer less than a minute. "Apparently not. She's in Savannah."

"Not anymore."

Cowboy spun around in the chair to face him. "Come again?"

Jesus. He'd never felt like such an idiot. "She was in Savannah, then I called her and left a message…"

"And?"

Jax shrugged. "And she disconnected the phone. Landlord said she left the next day."

"That doesn't make any sense. Why would she move again just because you called her?" He raised his eyebrows. "Are you that bad in bed?"

"Shut the fuck up, Leo."

Cowboy saluted. "Yes sir, mister commander man."

"Where the hell is she now?"

"It might take a week or two for her to show up. She needs to register with DMV, sign up for utilities, that sort of thing."

"It's already been over a month since she left Savannah."

"No wonder you've been such a dick." Cowboy's brows drew together. "She should be in here by now."

"She's not. There's no record of her anywhere in the country. It's like she doesn't exist anymore."

The news anchor on television filled the silence. "*An identity scandal has rocked the Savannah, Georgia, morgue. Ricky Kingfisher, a clerk in the morgue records office who previously served time for forging documents, is accused of selling the identities of unclaimed bodies from the morgue and allowing the victims to be buried as John and Jane Does.*"

Jax's eyes shot to the screen. "Jessa's maiden name is Kingfisher."

"How do you know that?"

"I was at the damn wedding."

Cowboy stood up next to Jax. "So, Jessa *Kingfisher* disappeared from Savannah right before Ricky *Kingfisher* got busted for selling new identities in the same town."

Jax's spine was tingling. "No. She wouldn't do it. She has no reason to take on a new identity."

"She had reason enough to move twice in two months. How do you explain that?"

Jax cursed under his breath. He'd foolishly assumed it was because of him. "She must be in some kind of trouble."

"It would explain why she's not showing up in our system."

"Contact the morgue," said Jax. "Find out the names that were stolen, and we can cross-reference them in our computer. Any women in their late twenties or early thirties, we check out."

"Will do." Cowboy turned to leave.

"And Leo, thanks."

"You got it, chief."

CHAPTER 7

ONLY ONE OF Ricky Kingfisher's stolen identities could possibly be Jessa, and Jax was on a flight to New Jersey within hours of his talk with Cowboy to investigate the lead.

It's not going to be her.

She wouldn't do such a thing.

He parked his rental car on the street. A few hundred feet ahead was a tiny bungalow that was rented to Maria Elena Cortez, who grew up in the Bronx, went to college at Clemson University, and recently relocated to New Jersey from Georgia.

Trouble was, Maria Elena was dead weeks before her most recent move.

Jessa wouldn't do it. Some other woman will answer the door.

He got out of his car, the tangy smell of saltwater

on the air. According to the morgue records confiscated by police, Maria Elena had been killed by an attacker in her apartment. With no next of kin, thieves in the Savannah morgue sold her identity to someone else and buried Maria in Potter's Field as a Jane Doe.

Jessa is not a criminal. She has no reason to buy someone else's identity.

Acid churned in Jax's stomach. He'd looked up Ricky Kingfisher and confirmed he was Jessa's first cousin. That was when his ulcer flared up. It was more than a coincidence that Jessa was missing and her cousin—who lived in the same town—was in the business of making people disappear.

Doubting Jessa made him think of his ex-wife. Jax knew what it felt like to find the person you thought you knew was actually a deceitful liar. He mentally chastised himself for grouping Jessa and Linda together and sincerely hoped the association was unjustified.

The white bungalow was nestled between a larger beach house on one side and a condominium complex on the other. The bungalow didn't belong here, standing out like Cinderella would have at the ball without the help of her fairy godmother, but parts of the Jersey Shore were like that.

He squinted against the sun to get a better view. There, along the edges of a small porch, were planters full of pink and purple flowers.

He cursed colorfully, even as a trace of excitement

laced his fury.

Jessa was in there.

She was in trouble. She must be.

What could be so bad that she would take on another woman's identity?

He knocked on the door, chastising the part of himself that was excited and raw. He was here because she was in trouble. He would not make this about the two of them and one night of mind-bending sex unless it was clear that was what she wanted, too.

CHAPTER 8

H E PEERED INSIDE. She didn't appear to be home.
The squawk of a seagull made him turn his head. There, just a few hundred feet away, was the public beach access point, and he was drawn to it—whether to look for Jessa or for his own peace of mind, he didn't know.

The first thing he saw as he crested the dunes was her long black hair blowing in the breeze.

His gut clenched.

Even from this distance he knew it was her. The surf grew louder as he approached its boundaries, the smell of the ocean heavy on the cool air. A smattering of people roamed the edge of the water, but his eyes were trained on Jessa as she stretched toward the sky with languid grace. She was a goddess, Venus herself, and he was drawn to her even as he hated himself for it.

He was close enough now to touch her and he reached out, the tendrils of her hair whipping his fingers. He let his hand drop. "Jessa."

She spun around and a look of pure horror came over her face. "What are you doing here? How did you find me?" She took a step back.

"I saw the morgue scandal on the news."

"What are you talking about?"

A group of teenagers walked by them, talking loudly, and Jax waited for them to pass. "Can we go inside?" he asked.

"No." She crossed her arms. "I'm not going anywhere with you."

Jax moved in close to her. "I'm the same person you've known for years, no matter what happened between us in that hotel room. So don't go acting like you're afraid of me, or I'm some big terrible person you can't stand."

"I don't want you here."

"I got that. But you're in trouble, and I came anyway." They'd attracted the attention of several people on the beach. "Now let's go inside. We need to talk."

"We can talk here."

He narrowed his eyes. "The things we need to talk about are better said indoors."

She stared at him for a moment and he could tell she wanted to say no, but instead she walked past him and picked up a blanket and book, then led the way back to her cottage.

He walked behind her, watching her round bottom sway from side-to-side within her white dress. The fabric was nearly see-through, and he could just make out her white underwear beneath it. Hard to believe the last time they'd seen each other, he'd been deep inside of her there.

She unlocked the door and he followed her into a tiny living room decorated in bright, bold colors and Mexican tile. She moved into the small but open kitchen, leaned against the counter, and crossed her arms. "What do you want?"

He followed her into the kitchen. "You're not going to make this easy on me, are you?"

"You're the one who's being difficult. Just say what you came here to say."

He took in the shadows under her eyes, the paleness of her skin. She didn't look well, though he still had the same reaction to her nearness he'd had two months before. "The police busted the identity theft ring where you got your fake ID."

"And?"

He narrowed his eyes. "You know your cousin worked in the morgue?"

She shrugged. "Sure. His parole officer got him the job last year."

"He was stealing the identities of unclaimed bodies,

then burying the people as Jane or John Does."

Her jaw dropped. "*What?*"

"I can see Ricky left that part out."

"Of course he did. I never would have knowingly participated in something like that."

"But if Maria Elena wasn't a real person, that would have been okay?"

She sucked her cheeks in. "Why are you here?"

He closed the distance between them. "It wouldn't have been okay with you. I know you better than that. You did it because you were desperate. What I don't understand is why."

"You don't know me at all." She ducked around him. "Get the hell out of here."

"What happened, Jessa?"

She turned on him. "What does it take to get away from you?"

"To get away from me?"

"I don't want you in my life. I don't want you to call me or follow me or contact me or look me up a year or five years down the road just to say hello."

"You got the message I left you in Savannah."

"Of course I got it, but I didn't want to talk to you. Yet here you are, chasing me across a dozen states despite that."

"It doesn't make sense." He followed her across the room. "Tell me why you would do such a stupid, crazy, illegal thing."

"You don't get to demand an explanation from me. We are nothing to each other. Nothing! Just because I got lonely and slept with you doesn't mean you matter to me. You are a mean-spirited, pompous asshole with no use for other people. Linda adored you, and even she couldn't stand to be around you for long. You couldn't truly care about a woman if your life depended on it."

The warmth he'd felt shining from her when they'd made love had defrosted some of the bitterness from his heart, but listening to her now made every fiber freeze solid. He'd been pining over a lost opportunity for love, but it was clear to him now she hated him.

Maybe she always had.

Then why the hell did she sleep with me?

She stormed past him, opening a door and taking a step inside. He could see it was a bedroom, and she was about to slam the door to separate them.

But she froze, standing unmoving for several seconds before she fell sideways in a dead faint.

CHAPTER 9

J AX HELD THE ice pack to Jessa's temple where she'd hit the corner molding when she fell, and tried to rouse her. He'd picked her up and brought her to the bed, and she hadn't even blinked.

That wasn't good.

Minutes passed before Jessa groaned and opened her eyes, immediately trying to sit up.

"Lie down," Jax said. "You took quite a fall."

She shook him off. "I don't want to lie down." Her eyes went around the bedroom and her face crumpled.

"What is it, Jessa?"

She raised her hand to point at the floor. "Those things were in my nightstand when I left for the beach this morning."

He looked at the collection of books, glasses, medicine, and tissues spread over the floor. "Just now? You mean someone was in here?"

She nodded. "It's the third time this week. The first was the worst. Drawers lying on the floor. Boxes emptied onto beds and tables. The first time, I thought it was just a burglary. Then I figured someone must have a key, so yesterday I changed the locks. Now I don't know what to think. Maybe they're looking for the person who used to live here."

Jax surveyed the room and was struck more by the lack of certain things than the inclusion of others.

There was no crib. There were no toys. This was the home of a woman who lived alone.

"There is no baby, is there?"

She swung her legs off the side of the bed. "You should go now."

"What happened?"

She turned on him. "What do you think happened, Jax? You're not stupid, so put two and two together and figure this one out."

She'd miscarried the baby.

All this time he'd told himself at least she had the child, some piece of Ralph to keep near her, when in fact she'd had nothing.

He remembered how happy she'd been about the baby, she and Ralph both. They were so clearly in love, their newly created family the perfect icing on the cake.

He'd been jealous at the time, his own marriage

going up in flames just before they announced they were expecting. Not that he missed Linda. More that he missed the woman he wanted Linda to be.

He wanted her to be more like Jessa.

Seeing her now, with her pain so clearly etched on her features, he recognized her loneliness like he reluctantly acknowledged his own. Difference being, he deserved to be unhappy. Jessa did not.

"I'm so sorry," he said, wishing he could wrap her in his arms and comfort her. Had she even had anyone there to do that at the time?

Her bottom lip trembled, then her mouth formed a hard line. "Please, Jax. Just leave."

"I can't do that."

"This is my house. It's my life. You don't get to stay here just because you want to."

"Because I want to? Someone broke into your house, not once but three times, most recently not an hour ago. What if they come back while you're sleeping, while you're alone?" He shook his head. "I'm staying."

"Where will you sleep? There's only one bed and you can't sleep with me." She lowered her brow.

Was that why she didn't want him here? "I'll sleep on the sofa."

"There is no sofa."

"Then I'll sleep on the floor."

"This is ridiculous. I can take care of myself."

"You passed out when you saw they'd been here, Jessa. I'm not leaving you alone like this."

Not this time.

I won't let you suffer alone again.

She closed her eyes. "Fine. Just for tonight, but after that you need to leave."

He nodded. "We'll talk about it in the morning."

CHAPTER 10

J ESSA WIPED THE fog off the washroom mirror and looked at her naked body. Her breasts were noticeably bigger, their peaks darker and seemingly larger as well. She ran her hands around them, checking their firmness and weight. Could Jax see the differences that were so obvious to her eyes?

Her hands moved lower, caressing the skin over her lower abdomen that had begun to stretch over her growing belly. She was nearing the end of her first trimester, and naked like this, she was surely beginning to show.

It's nothing my clothes won't hide.

As long as Jax didn't see her naked, she had nothing to worry about, and there was no chance in hell of that happening.

She pulled her panties up over her legs and settled

them in place. She was so aware of herself as a woman while he was here, and she didn't like the feeling one bit. She'd been happy at the beach, at least until the first break-in. Content to live quietly in the cute little house and let her baby grow, but Jax's arrival had changed all that.

She slipped her thin nightgown over her head and walked into the bedroom then climbed into bed and pulled up her covers. He had no right to be here. He shouldn't have been able to find her at all, yet here he was, refusing to leave and insisting on protecting her.

Her eyes closed as she settled into the mattress. The slightest noise at the window had her sitting upright, her heart racing. It was nothing, she was sure.

Okay, if she was being completely honest, she felt far better with him being here than she had without, especially given today's break-in. Jax had determined the burglar had entered through the bedroom window right at the foot of the bed, and though the window was locked now and the curtains pulled, she knew full well she'd never get to sleep without him in the house tonight.

What about after tonight?

God, she couldn't stomach the idea of moving again. She'd been so tired lately, to boot, and moving one more time seemed like more than she could handle. But what other choice did she have? Stay here, where someone was determined to break into her cottage every chance they got, or let Jax stay on as her live-in bodyguard?

Over my dead body.

A knock at her bedroom door had her heart pounding. "Yes?"

He poked his head in the door. "I'm going outside to look around."

"Is everything okay?"

"Yeah. Get some sleep."

She was certainly tired, but she wondered if she would in fact be able to rest, partly because of whoever tried to break in and partly because of her bodyguard. He disrupted her entire world with his presence, not only because of the threat he posed to her child but because of the threat he posed to her inflamed emotions.

Everything made her cry these days. She was cranky and needy and desperate for company. She was a nurse, but Maria Elena held no such certification, so even her passion for her work had to be sacrificed in this game. She'd been working at the local library, a job that didn't lend itself to conversation.

Now that Jax had found her, she could go back to being herself, back to caring for people as she loved to do. That was some consolation, at least.

It will be great. You can work on the weekends when Jax has custody of the baby.

The urge to cry came quickly and wouldn't be

denied. Curling onto her side, she let the tears come. She'd worked so hard to escape him, gone to such lengths and extremes, yet here he was. If she couldn't convince him to leave her alone, she had only to wait for the day he discovered the truth and laid claim to the baby he'd unknowingly created.

And when that day came, only one thing was certain. Jax was going to hate her, and would become an inescapable part of her life from that moment forward.

CHAPTER 11

J AX STEPPED INTO the cold night air, his Glock at
his side and his night-vision monocular in his
hand. The surf crashed in the distance, the scent of the
air salty and sharp. He used his monocular to survey
his surroundings. The path to the beach was deserted.

He moved to the side of the house, taking in the
balconies of the condo complex and a hundred feet of
vegetated sand dunes between Jessa's house and the
complex. The other side of her property was open to a
neighbor, with nowhere to hide, so clearly it was the
dune side of the structure he had to be concerned with.

He made his way to the dunes, his mind lost in
thought as he walked. He hadn't anticipated the depth
of Jessa's dislike toward him. Her words rang out in his
memory.

You are a mean-spirited, pompous asshole with no use for

other people.

Hell, he could have said as much about himself, but hearing it out of her mouth was something else entirely. Because he did have a use for her. He had a whole host of uses just waiting to be explored, and it wasn't just about sex. Damn it, he liked her—and he didn't like anybody.

Still, he'd protect her. He'd stay here as long as he needed to, to make sure she was safe. He'd left Hawk in charge of HERO Force, and they didn't need everyone on the mission they were doing this week. Besides, sleeping on the floor would be good for him. Help to get the message through his thick damn skull that Jessa didn't want anything to do with him.

Jessa.

Why had she taken on a new identity? Maybe she was in trouble. Money trouble, or…something. But he just couldn't imagine what trouble Jessa could get into.

A hundred feet from the dunes, movement caught his eye. The grass was moving as if someone was crawling through it, and the hair on Jax's arms stood up on end as he continued to walk and raised his monocular to his eye once more. There in the brush was a man crawling away on his stomach.

Jax reached for his Glock as he began to run toward the figure. The other man stood and ran, too, a large shape at his side. Jax was gaining on him, but the man made it to a parking lot and an SUV, speeding away just as Jax got to him.

"Son of a bitch!" yelled Jax. He doubled back to the dune and the brush area where the man had been, quickly locating his hideout by the flattened foliage behind a large swath of tall grass. He dropped into a squat to examine the area with a flashlight. A pattern of distinctive and familiar markings was left in the sand.

The tripod of a sniper's rifle. He turned and looked back at her house, the kitchen window shining brightly in the night.

Whoever was watching Jessa's house was looking for something and was willing to kill in order to find it.

He couldn't let that happen.

Jesus.

What had she gotten herself into?

Some kind of trouble, that was for damn sure, and she wasn't talking. It was time for him to find some answers, with or without her cooperation.

Back at the bungalow, he closed all the drapes and locked both doors, then turned his attention to Jessa's belongings. He went through every drawer, cupboard, and box she had in the kitchen and living room, as well as a hallway closet.

What could they possibly be looking for?

In one box he found scrapbooks of her wedding and life with Ralph. Her diplomas. A small desk in the corner held mail and bills, and he scrupulously checked for anything amiss financially but found nothing. If anything, Ralph had left her enough money that she shouldn't have any issues at all.

One envelope caught his attention, with the return address of a lawyer's office.

I write to inform you of certain assets bequeathed to you pursuant to Mr. Hopewell's Last Will and Testament, to wit: a first edition copy of The Manor *by John Boronkay.*

So Jessa had inherited a book that was meant for Maria Elena.

"What do you think you're doing?" Jessa exclaimed.

He twisted around and saw her standing in a white fuzzy bathrobe, indignation clearly etched on her features. "Trying to figure out what's going on, since you aren't going to tell me."

"You have no right to go through my things!"

He stood up and faced her. "I need all the information so I can figure out who's after you and what they want. If you don't like that, you can try being honest with me."

She huffed.

"That's what I thought," he said. "Where's the book you inherited from"—he looked back at the lawyer's letter—"Harold Hopewell?"

She looked around the room, selecting the old-looking volume and handing it to him. "Here. I was reading it at the beach today."

"When did you get this letter?"

"Two weeks ago. Why?"

"And when was the first break-in?"

"Ten days ago. Do you think they're related?"

"Can you think of any reason someone would be interested in something of yours?"

"No. None."

He held the book in his hands, twisting it back and forth in the light. "Then this might have something to do with it. What's it about?"

"A wealthy family in New England."

"Maybe Harold Hopewell was in love with Maria Elena Cortez."

"Maybe, but with a name like Harold I think he might be older." She sat down. "It still makes me sick to know she was a real person, and I stole a proper burial from her. I should have realized when the book arrived. I just figured they had me mistaken for somebody else."

Jax dialed his phone. "Logan, I need you to pull everything you can find on one Harold Hopewell."

Jessa pulled at his arm. "No. I don't want you to do this."

"He died a few weeks ago, his lawyer's in Boston, firm by the name of Layton, Felder, Bach & Moore."

"Stop it," said Jessa. "I don't want HERO Force involved."

"Hang on." Jax pulled the phone from his ear.

"We need information. Logan can get it."

"I don't care. I don't want anything to do with you or your men."

He glared at her and put the phone back to his ear. "It's a rush job. Let me know what you find out."

Jessa hit his shoulder as he hung up. "I hate you. Do you know that?"

He narrowed his eyes. "Sort of begs the question, why did you sleep with me?"

"You need to leave. I've had enough of this cloak-and-dagger garbage."

"You're right. We should go."

She held up her hands. "I'm not going anywhere."

"I can't protect you here, Jessa."

"I don't need protection. This is just a couple of kids—"

"There was a man hiding in the brush of the sand dunes. One man, alone."

Her eyes went wide.

Jax put his hands on his hips. "He ran when I got close to him. He had a sniper rifle, and he was pointing it at your house, looking through the scope and watching you."

Jessa grabbed her throat, a look of pure fear settling over her features.

"That weapon has one purpose and one purpose only," said Jax. "To end your life. I figure either he's after the book or he has something to do with the reason you wanted a new identity in the first place. You need to come clean with me, Jessa. This isn't a game."

"You think I don't know that? You think I want this to be happening to me?"

"Then why aren't you telling me everything? You're keeping secrets and they just might get you killed."

Her bottom lip trembled.

"You can trust me with anything. Don't you know that?" he asked. "Why did you need a new identity?"

She turned away. "None of your business."

He closed his eyes and bit out his words. "We're leaving. Get your things, and make sure you bring that book."

CHAPTER 12

J ESSA CLUTCHED HER bag close to her chest as she
sat beside Jax in his truck. She didn't want to be
here. She turned her head and watched the mile
markers flash in the headlights. Anything but talk to
this man.

It was bad enough she was stuck here, sharing the
same air. With the pregnancy, she was overly sensitive
to smells, and the smell of Jax was ubiquitous in the
truck cab. She cracked the window, ignoring him as he
sent her a questioning look.

"How's your head?" he asked.

"Fine."

"Any headache?"

She sighed. "I said it's fine."

He rubbed his hand up and down his denim-clad
thigh. "Mind if I put on some music?"

"Your truck."

"Did I do something to make you angry?"

She turned her head and stared at him. "Seriously?"

"If I did, I don't know what it is, so why don't you tell me?"

She clutched her purse more tightly. "Hunting me down like a stalker. Going through my things without asking. And to top it all off, I don't want to be here with you."

"I'm trying to keep you safe."

"No one asked you to do that."

Jax glared at her. "Oh, so I was just supposed to leave you in that beach house with a sniper outside your goddamn window?"

"I'm a grown woman. If you left me there, I would have gotten somewhere safe on my own. I am not alive at this very moment because of you."

"Do you have your own team of guys working to find out who's after you? Because if HERO Force's efforts are redundant, I can certainly find something else for them to work on, like the protection detail I just turned down for an election in Central America."

"Then go ahead, Jax."

He shook his head. "What the hell's the matter with you, huh? I'm busting my ass to do what I can to help you here—"

"When all I want is for you to go away."

"You certainly didn't want me to go away the last time I saw you."

Jessa sank down a little in her seat. She didn't want to be reminded of what happened between them, beyond her extracting some kind of justice from him for Ralph and the baby.

She didn't want to remember how she'd responded to him.

She blushed, her cheeks burning. A sliver of memory slipped through her armor, Jax on top of her as she keened, clutching his body deep into hers. The only time she usually thought of that night was when her conscious mind went to sleep and the dreams took over. They were vivid and sharp, a blend of actual moments from inside that hotel room and the wildest imaginings of her hormone-laden mind.

"Why did you make love with me, Jessa?"

"It was sex, and I told you, I was lonely. You were there."

He was quiet after that, and she felt like she was waiting for a geyser to explode. The calmness at the surface masked a firestorm beneath that was bound to shoot forth with hot, burning scorn.

When he did speak, his voice was quiet. "You can pretend, if that's what you want. You can pretend it could have been any man with you in that bed, but I know better. You came to me looking for something mechanical, impersonal. But that's not what you got, and pretending you didn't enjoy making love to me is a lie neither one of us believes."

His deep voice reverberated through her body, the truck now uncomfortably warm. She put her window down more. God, she needed to get out of here.

He was right, she knew he was, and the truth of it fueled her anger. He'd taken something from her that night—her identity as a grieving widow—and like a coat in a cold winter storm, she had no idea what to do without it.

Except freeze.

Jax said, "Why did you change your identity?"

"None of your business."

"Damn it, Jessa, I want to help you, but I can't do that if you don't tell me what's going on. You must have been terrified to do something so drastic. Something happened that scared you enough to do something desperate. Did someone hurt you?"

"No."

"Threaten you?"

"No."

"Blackmail you?"

"Stop it, Jax. I don't want you to help me. Don't you get that? I don't need a hero. I need you to leave me alone and stay out of my life."

"I owe Ralph more than that."

"You owe Ralph the rest of his life with his wife and child, but it's too late for you to pay what you owe."

Jax slowed down and took an exit ramp off the highway.

"I wish it hadn't happened, Jessa. I wish I could go back in time and change the decisions I made that day, but I can't. Ralph knew the risks when he went in there. We all did."

Her eyes began to burn. "Then why didn't you go? Huh? How come you're alive and my husband is dead?"

He didn't answer, and she pushed at his shoulder. "How come you didn't send someone else in there, someone who didn't have a family waiting for him to come home?" She pushed him again, harder this time.

Jax pulled to the side of the road and turned to her, holding up his hands. "I made the best decision I could at the time with the information I had available to me."

"Fuck you!" She was swinging wildly now, her fists connecting with skin and bone. "I hate you so much. I wish it was you who died that night, not my Ralph!"

She was sobbing, great gasping breaths and shudders racking her body as she tried to hurt him. Then she was just crying, tears streaming down her face as she cried out, years of pain and anguish coming out of her body like a spirit in an exorcism.

Then his arms were around her, his shoulder beneath her head, his body squeezing hers, and it felt so good to be comforted, so good to say the horrible things that had been festering inside her for too long. And even as she hated that it was Jax who was holding her, she knew no other man could release this burden. It had to be him, and that truth tethered her to him as surely as a physical chain.

She wiped her cheek on his shoulder and sniffed. He smelled good to her now instead of stifling as he had before, the warmth of his body carrying the spicy cinnamon scent that was uniquely his own.

They stayed like that, locked together, until the last of the shudders left her breath and the shoulder of his shirt was soaked from her tears.

Embarrassment began to creep into her awareness, and she lifted her head, scooting back to her side of the bench seat. "Sorry."

"It's okay. You have every right to feel the way you do."

She looked out her window, her gaze catching on her own reflection, illuminated by the dashboard lights. Who was this woman, sitting in the dark with Jax Andersson, carrying his child? How had she gotten from the grieving widow to a person capable of doing such a thing?

"We need to stop for the night," Jax said. "There's a motel right up here."

"Fine."

He started the truck and drove to the motel, getting

out to check in and coming back for her. "There's only one room available. A king suite. I'll sleep on the floor."

She didn't answer, but her eyes squeezed shut. There would be no reprieve from this man tonight, and she desperately needed space. Time to herself to lick the wounds of this day, time to shore herself up for the days ahead. She had so much to think about, so much to consider, and none of it could be done with Jax sharing her space.

She followed him to the room, remembering the last time she'd followed him to a hotel room, only this time she was tired and beleaguered and worn.

He opened the door and held it for her, cold air from the air conditioner blasting her in the face.

Did he remember that, too? She snuck a glance at him, only to find him staring at her intently.

He remembered, all right.

"I'm going to take a shower," she said, anxious to put a locked door between herself and this man. Closing it behind her, she leaned up against it and shut her eyes. When she opened them, she looked at herself in the mirror.

Yelling at Jax in the car—telling him how she blamed him for Ralph's death—was cathartic and exhausting. But what surprised her was her own reaction to the words being ripped from her chest.

She recognized her tirade from the days she spent

in counseling following Ralph's death. The stages of grief, her counselor had said. Blaming. Accepting. She couldn't remember the others right now. But the accusations she'd flung at Jax were the stuff grief brochures were made of.

"I will never accept it," she whispered to her reflection. Her anger at Jax Andersson was nothing she intended to get over.

Climbing into the shower, she felt herself relax— every muscle that had been clenched too tightly and shoulder that had been held too high seeming to drop in an instant. She ran a hand over her lower abdomen. "It was a long day today, huh, Baby? Don't you worry about a thing. You just grow big and strong in there. I'll take care of…"

Your daddy.

Her eyes popped open wide, but she focused on nothing. "Him."

She let the water run over her until her fingers pruned and reluctantly turned off the water. She dried her body and put on one of two fresh outfits she'd brought with her before bracing herself to face Jax again.

He was lying back on the bed like a Greek god on a cloud, and she hated that she noticed how attractive he was.

"I got us some snacks," he said. On the bed was a bottle of Cabernet Sauvignon and a package of pretzels. "That's what you like, right?" he asked.

Her favorites, actually, and the wine would have gone a long way toward relieving her discomfiture if she could drink it. She took the pretzels. "I'm surprised you remember."

"I remember lots of things."

She looked away, not wanting to encourage the look she saw smoldering in his eyes.

"I remember how you like your coffee," he said. "Cream, no sugar. And I remember you like to wake up early and go walking by yourself."

He seemed to be waiting for her to say something, but she stared intently into her pretzel bag, ignoring the fluttering of her heartbeat and the liquid shimmer of his words on the air.

He rolled toward her side of the bed. "I remember how you lay in a hammock with one leg trailing on the ground and the other up high by the knot. I remember the big smile on your face when you ride a bike, like you're a kid who just figured out how to do it. But more than anything else, I remember your laugh."

Somewhere between coffee and bike rides she'd stopped breathing.

Jax touched her face. "You have the most beautiful laugh. I want to hear it again someday."

Jessa swallowed a pretzel, forcing the dryness past her knotted throat. She thought of everything she wanted in this moment and everything she didn't want.

The things she couldn't deal with. "Please don't be nice to me tonight," she whispered.

"Why not?"

"I don't think I can take it."

He stared at her for a moment, and she wondered what he was thinking. He sat up. "I'm going to shower, too."

Disappointment curled in her stomach and she silently cursed her ambivalence before scurrying under the covers and opening the book. What was so special about this book that made it important enough to break into her house for?

Unlike Jax, she knew the book must be the reason for the break-ins, and she was determined to read as much as she could tonight in hopes she could answer that question.

CHAPTER 13

J AX HAD THE water on as hot as it would go, the
heat seeping into his tight neck muscles and
melting the tension away. His mind replayed the scene
with Jessa in his truck that night, her all-consuming
anger and the blame she placed squarely at his feet.

What he'd told her was true. Ralph did know the
danger that awaited him at Steele's mansion, but that
didn't make her assessment any less correct. He was
responsible for Ralph's death. He'd always known that.

And now he desperately wanted Ralph's wife. He
wanted her in the cab of his truck when she cried and
beat on him. He wanted her just now in the bedroom
when she told him she couldn't handle what was
happening between them. He wanted her even more
now than he did the night they'd made love.

What kind of person did that make him?

He closed his eyes against the searing spray. He'd always thought she was beautiful. But now things were different, more complicated, and he was far more culpable than he'd ever been before.

Because it wasn't just sex. And it wasn't just a preoccupation with her physical beauty. He wanted Jessa, and not just in his bed. He thought of Ralph and mumbled under his breath, "I hope it's okay with you." He rubbed his hands over his eyes. "She hates my guts, if it's any consolation." He turned off the water.

After seeing the depth of Jessa's feelings, he didn't understand why she'd come to him. Hatred and lust were particularly strange bedfellows, though there was no denying the chemistry between them.

When they'd walked down the corridor toward the room tonight, it was like déjà vu. Then the air conditioning had blasted them with cold air, and he was right back there, Jessa standing before him, so skittish he thought she might bolt.

He tugged on his jeans and opened the bathroom door, steam wafting out around him in the cold room. Jessa was already asleep, the book on her chest as if she'd been reading, and he took it and put it on the nightstand.

Despite everything she'd said to him today, he still wanted her, and he allowed himself to wonder what would happen if he woke her up with kisses.

She'd probably punch me in the face.

Moving to the other side of the bed, he took a pillow and a spare blanket from the closet and settled on the floor. He fell asleep listening to the rise and fall of Jessa's breathing, his mind replaying the familiar tape of the two of them making love.

Imagining what could have happened tonight if she'd been willing.

He wasn't sure what woke him.

Sitting up, Jax took in the hotel room, his memory quickly returning.

"My baby," mumbled Jessa.

He stood up and walked to her side of the bed, guilt like a familiar drink he had sipped too often. She was still dreaming of the baby she lost, and he ached for her as he sat on the edge of the bed and lightly stroked her hair.

"You'll have another baby someday, sweetheart," he whispered.

She swatted at his hand. "She's mine!"

He jostled her shoulder. "Jessa, it's just a dream. Wake up."

She opened her eyes and stared at him blankly.

"You were dreaming," he said.

Her brows drew together, her eyes wide open. "You can't have her. I'm her mother."

"Okay, you can have her," he agreed, and Jessa leaned back against the pillows.

"No visibation," she said.

He smiled at her slurred speech. "Right. No visibation."

He climbed back under his own covers.

No visitation?

His eyes popped open. She was dreaming of fighting over a child. Not actual history, after all. He rolled onto his side. Jessa seemed to be under a tremendous amount of stress right now, and clearly her mind wasn't giving her any break.

CHAPTER 14

J ESSA WAS SITTING with her legs curled up on the bench seat and her arms wrapped around her middle. If Jax didn't know better, he'd think she was sick, but she insisted she was fine.

"I don't understand what you think the lawyers can tell you," she said.

"I have a hunch that Maria Elena's death wasn't a random event. We know whoever was stalking your beach house was armed with a sniper rifle, so we have to consider the possibility the real Maria Elena was killed by the same person who's after you."

"What, she was murdered?"

Jax nodded. "By an intruder. Cops said it was likely a burglary in progress, but she lived alone, so there was no way to tell if anything was actually taken."

"What do you think?"

"I think whoever wants that book killed Maria Elena so she'd never receive it. Only the lawyers from Harold Hopewell's estate can tell us what would have happened if Maria Elena hadn't risen from the dead. If they sent the inheritance to her, but she wasn't alive to receive it, what would have happened to that package?"

"You think the next heir in line is the killer."

"Exactly. And the person who's after you." Jax stared in his rearview mirror. "Don't turn around, but we've got a tail. They've been following us since we left the hotel."

"How can you tell?"

"They're always two cars behind us. Never right behind, but twice now I've sped up and they catch up, then get two cars behind. When I stopped for gas, they stopped, too, but no one got out of the car. They want me to know they're there."

"What do we do?"

"I haven't figured that out yet." He took a sip of his coffee. "Aren't you going to drink yours?" He'd gotten her a double espresso at the gas station, something he knew she liked, but he was nearly done with his cup and she had yet to touch hers.

"I gave it up. If there is someone following us, they must have been following us yesterday, too."

"Not necessarily. I would have noticed if they were. Hang on." He cut across two lanes of traffic to exit at a rest stop that advertised a McDonald's and a Starbucks Coffee.

Jessa turned around. "They kept going."

Jax parked the truck and turned to her. "There must be a transmitter on something. What did you bring with you?"

"Just my purse and the book."

"Let me see your purse."

"I don't think…"

He picked it up off the floor. "We're looking for something small, probably plastic but it could be metal." He began digging through the contents of her purse. Within moments, he withdrew a cube slightly smaller than an old flash bulb. "Bingo."

"That's not mine," she said.

"A GPS transmitter. It's reporting our location as we speak. These are professionals, not amateurs, Jessa."

Maybe even professional hit men.

The thought was unsettling.

Jessa held the transmitter in her palm. "Whoever broke into the house must have put it there."

"My guess is, we're going to find our dark sedan within a mile or two of this rest stop, pulled over with imaginary car trouble and waiting for us."

"What do we do now?"

Jax looked around the parking lot. "We find a rest stop employee who didn't bother to lock his car. Sit tight. I'll be right back."

He made his way briskly across the parking lot to a row of cars set apart from the masses of highway traffic. The second car he tried was unlocked, and the gate pass he was looking for was tucked neatly under the visor.

He climbed back in next to Jessa, handing her the card. "This will get us out the backside of the rest stop through the employee entrance. Our tail is going to take awhile to catch up to us once he realizes where we've gone."

He reached for his drink, only to find them both missing. "What happened to my coffee?"

"I threw it away. That much caffeine isn't good for you."

"You threw out my coffee?"

"Why don't we just throw the GPS in a trash can, too, so this person stops following us?"

"Because it's time to find out who's after you, and we're going to use the GPS as bait." He swung around behind the rest stop service building. "You're lucky we're in a hurry, or I'd run inside Starbucks and buy two more." He shook his head. "Who throws away someone else's coffee?"

CHAPTER 15

J ESSA'S STOMACH WAS refusing to settle this morning, even after she'd dumped the coffee. The smell that had started her insides cartwheeling was still threatening to turn into something far more disgusting.

She watched as Jax unpacked his weapons from the bed of the truck. Rifle cases, pistol cases, a small box that looked a lot like a briefcase. That one probably held the explosives. She closed her eyes and shimmied her shoulders, a cold breeze seeming to blow through her.

She'd grown up around guns, and Ralph certainly owned more than his fair share. There'd even been a time when she enjoyed shooting, but that was before she was married to Ralph and saw him come home twice with bullet wounds. That was enough to make her shy away from guns.

She didn't want anything to do with HERO Force. There had been a time in her life when she thought it was an admirable organization, when she thought the men who earned their living working for it were a special breed.

Now she just thought they were crazy.

Why else would a man put everything and everyone he cared about on a back burner? Why else would the man she loved have put HERO Force before her happiness?

She hadn't gotten over it. Hadn't moved on, hadn't found some way to forgive him. She hadn't become the person she used to be, and dammit, she was angry. Angry that Ralph was dead, and that a part of her had died with him.

She hadn't wanted him to go on that mission to Steele's house. But had he listened to her? Of course not. He listened to the almighty HERO Force instead, and the commands of their fearless leader, Jax Andersson.

Now here she was with Jax experiencing all of the same things she had experienced with Ralph, fighting all of the same battles she had thought were behind her, and she was highly aware of the baby in her belly who needed her protection and a safe, quiet life.

The exact opposite of everything HERO Force stood for.

Jax opened the rifle case and took out a weapon.

He met her stare. "Do you know how to shoot?"

"Yes."

"Do you want the Glock or the rifle?"

Jessa closed her eyes. "Neither."

"Our tail should be here momentarily. I might need some help from you."

She thought of the baby in her belly and longed to find safety away from this place.

You'll never be safe so long as this person is trying to kill you.

Jax eyed her warily. "I have no idea what we're going to be up against here, Jessa. I might need you armed."

"I'll take the Glock." She inspected the magazine.

"It's like riding a bike. It will come back to you."

"Except a bike is more fun and doesn't kill any-body."

"Right. Except for that." He winked at her, and she felt a flash of annoyance.

"How long do you think we have?" she asked.

"A few minutes, at least. If this guy is coming after you with a weapon, you pull the trigger. Do you hear me?" A gust of wind blew her hair in her face and she flipped it back, pretending not to notice the way Jax looked at her when she did.

Jax began to walk. "Let's get into the trees and find a good place to hide."

She walked quickly behind him, suddenly feeling very unsafe in the clearing, panic rising within her like a quickly burning fire.

Jax hopped over a large felled tree, then held out his hand to help her across. "We'll be safe here. At least for starters."

"Well, that's super comforting."

Jax chuckled. "I said it just to make you feel better, too."

Jessa kneeled down in the brush, a spongy layer of damp leaves wicking moisture onto her pants and the earthy smell of the forest surrounding her. She imagined this was what a hunter must feel like.

Better the hunter than the hunted.

She said a silent prayer for their safety, suddenly fearful for herself and her child. If Jax knew she was pregnant, he never would have asked her to arm herself and watch his back. But who did he have besides her to do it?

Jax turned to her, his face utterly calm and in control. "You stay here. God willing, I'll be doing this alone. But if he comes for you, use your weapon. Don't be afraid of this bastard, Jessa."

She nodded curtly. "You already said that." The sound of an approaching vehicle could be heard in the distance.

"Get down now."

She did as she was told, pressing her body against the trunk, only vaguely aware of the rotting bark and damp mold against her skin. She was focused on the metal in her hand, the butt of the Glock seemingly the only sure thing in existence.

Jax moved ten feet away to a large bush. She looked at him questioningly, and he gestured for her to stay put.

He doesn't want to be near me, in case the bad guy gets too close.

She swallowed hard against the dryness in her throat, refusing to let herself think about what that might mean. In the clearing below, a car came into view, circling once before stopping.

The driver got out.

He was short, with whitish-blond hair that blew in the breeze, and for a moment she thought he looked harmless. He spun around once, slowly, then he went back in his car and retrieved a large semiautomatic weapon. Jessa's stomach danced, and she wished she'd been sick already so maybe the nausea would leave her alone.

You have to be strong. Two of you are going to walk out of these woods, and that man isn't one of them.

They just had to wait.

Another gust of wind blew through the trees. With these conditions, he had to be closer for Jax to aim reliably. He would get one shot that had the benefit of surprise. Anything after that would be a battle.

So they waited as the white-haired man slowly got closer.

Jessa was bent over behind the log, holding herself at an uncomfortable angle. The muscles of her arms straining to keep herself still were suddenly too fatigued to continue, and her torso shifted an inch or two to the right. The bullet came so quickly she nearly gasped out loud, bark flying off the tree that hid her.

Then Jax was firing, the rounds coming in quick succession, and she knew they were shooting at each other. She closed her eyes. She couldn't handle another one of them dying. Had barely survived the first. It occurred to her their odd little family was under fire—mother, child, unwitting father.

A body hit the ground, the man grunting as he fell. She couldn't tell if it was Jax or their stalker.

She was trembling, shaking in her own skin, fear for Jax and fear for her own safety intertwining. If it was Jax who remained standing, he would call to her. He would let her know.

But he did not call, and with every passing second, the certainty he was dead sank into her flesh like the most vicious acid. She'd lost them both. Ralph and Jax were both dead now.

The sound of footsteps approaching the log had her eyes opening wide. Terror and adrenaline surged through her system. There was no one to save her now except herself. No one to protect her baby except its mother.

She trained her weapon over the log, her eyes making contact with the man. He raised his arm to fire, but she got off one shot before he could. He kept coming, the sound of his approach now slowed and echoing in her ears in slow motion.

Damn it! How long had it been since she fired a weapon? How long since she'd worked to hit a target from any real kind of distance? The gun in her hand would only defend her if she could aim it well.

She could hear Ralph's voice in her head, reminding her to brace the gun on the log and look down the barrel, but to do that she would need to put her head in her attacker's line of fire.

Show me another way.

The loud screech of a bird made her look up. A bald eagle flew overhead and straight for the shooter, who had no choice but to shoo it away, his attention now completely off of Jessa.

She propped the Glock on top of the log and looked down the barrel. The white-haired man realized his mistake a moment before she fired, his jaw dropping as she pulled the trigger.

A black dot appeared in the middle of his forehead. He swayed, then fell to the ground. The eagle landed on the forest floor just ten feet from Jessa.

"Ralph?" she whispered. The bird tilted its head.

Jessa's mouth pulled down hard at the corners. "Thank you."

It stayed and stared at her for a beat, then flew

away, its majestic wings lifting it high into the sky.

I have to find Jax.

She spun in a circle, frantically searching for him, then began running and calling his name, weaving in and out of trees, brush, and boulders. She finally spotted him on his side beneath a large tree nearly covered in brush.

He was not moving.

"Jax!" She was frantically pulling at him, tugging his body out from under the brush. Where was he hit? Was he already dead? She heard sobbing and realized it was coming from her own mouth.

Her hands found the blood at the back of his head, warm and sticky and saturating his hair, and hoped the large rock beside him was to blame and not a bullet.

"Jax! Can you hear me? I need you to wake up now."

She made a fist with her hand and rubbed her knuckles along his sternum, deliberately causing him pain. His eyes opened as he moaned.

"Jax, you have to wake up!"

His eyes met hers, consciousness clear in their depths, and he winced. "You okay?" he asked.

"Yes."

"The tango?"

She gestured toward the dead man.

He leveled his stare on her. "You did that?"

She nodded, not yet able to comprehend that she'd

taken a life. There'd be time for that later, when they weren't standing so close to their own mortality.

"Good job." He sat up, his face scrunching into a wince.

"Are you hit?" she asked.

He felt around his arms and chest. "I don't think so."

"Your shoulder," she said, noticing the blood that was seeping through his shirt. "Let me see." Gingerly, she lifted the fabric from his wound and looked beneath it. "It's a flesh wound. It needs to be bandaged, and you probably have a concussion from the rock you landed on."

He grabbed on to a tree branch and pulled himself to a stand. "I'm fine. Let's hit the road."

"At least let me drive. And we need to stop and get supplies to take care of your wound."

"You're pretty cute when you worry about me."

"Don't call me cute."

"Fine. Just don't go all Florence Nightingale on me, batting your eyes and hoping I notice."

She opened her mouth and glared at him. He was smiling, and he winked. He put his arm around her. "It's okay now, Jessa. Everything's going to be okay."

CHAPTER 16

THE LAW OFFICES of Layton, Felder, Bach & Moore were in the center of downtown Boston and screamed of old money.

"Just follow my lead," whispered Jax in Jessa's ear as they were escorted into a conference room, a large painting of a mansion overlooking the ocean hanging in an ornate gold frame on the longest wall.

Jessa stared at it as they waited for the lawyer to join them, rubbing one hand over the other.

She'd killed a man today.

There would be gunpowder on her hands from firing the gun. She wondered absently if it would wash off, or if days from now someone could test her hands for the chemicals and see what she'd done.

If only the experience would wash away as easily as the gun powder.

It was necessary, she knew, and given the same circumstance a hundred times, a hundred times she'd kill him. But somehow that didn't make it much easier to swallow.

When Ralph was a SEAL and later with HERO Force, she wouldn't allow herself to think of the deaths her husband was responsible for. When he came home with injuries, she never once asked what the other guy looked like, or what harm Ralph had done.

She didn't like to think about people causing death, and now she was one of them. She rubbed her trigger finger with her opposite hand.

"You okay?" asked Jax.

"No."

He put his hand on her forearm. "Thank you for what you did today."

She turned and met his eyes. "You didn't see him, did you?"

"Who?"

"The eagle. He swooped in and distracted the shooter so I could set up my shot."

"An eagle?"

She nodded. "A bald eagle. Just like on the SEAL insignia. Without him we'd both be dead."

A knowing look settled over Jax's features. "He helped you."

"He helped us."

The conference room door opened and a man in a

suit and tie walked in. "Good afternoon. I'm Fred Bach. What can I do for you, Mr. Andersson?"

"This is Maria Elena Cortez. She received a package from your law firm a few weeks ago with a book bequeathed to her from Mr. Harold Hopewell."

"Yes, Mr. Hopewell has been a client here at Layton, Felder, Bach & Moore for many, many years. It was an honor to execute his final wishes."

Jax leaned forward in his chair. "I was hoping you could answer a few questions for me about Mr. Hopewell's will."

The lawyer frowned. "Once the person is deceased, their last will and testament becomes a matter of public record. Now, it can take some time for those documents to make their way down to the courthouse, or the records room, but the public is entitled to know what was written inside them."

Jax nodded. "Great, then we shouldn't have any problems getting some answers."

"What exactly are you looking for?" asked the lawyer.

"I want to know what would have happened if Maria Elena hadn't been alive and well to receive this package from your law firm."

The lawyer furrowed his brow. "That's an odd question. May I ask why you're interested?"

"Someone broke into my home," said Jessa. "I believe they were looking for the book."

"I see." Fred walked behind his desk and opened a file. "So you're thinking someone with a vested interest in the estate may have had something to do with that."

"Yes," she said.

"Actually, in this case, we had some trouble locating Ms. Cortez. The address we had on file for her was no longer valid, and we needed to hire a private investigator to track her down. It was several weeks before we were able to locate you, Ms. Cortez."

"But what would have happened if you hadn't been able to find me?"

"Well, according to the provisions of the will, if the inheritance is returned to our law firm as undeliverable and we are unable to locate the heir, then the inheritance would be passed on to another beneficiary."

Jax raised an eyebrow. "And who might that beneficiary be?"

The lawyer tilted his head and folded his hands across the file. "I'm not certain I should share that information at this time."

"If it's a matter of public record, then what difference does it make?"

"Technically it's a matter of public record. Realistically, if you went through legal means to obtain this information, it would take you a minimum of several weeks from today to get it." He smiled a small smile. "Mr. Hopewell was a very good client. I feel it's our duty to protect the dignity of his Last Will and

Testament."

Jax and Jessa exchanged a look. Jessa rested her elbow on the armrest and cocked an eyebrow at the lawyer. "It wasn't just the break-ins. Someone is trying to hurt me."

The lawyer's eyes went wide. "Excuse me?"

"Maybe even kill me. They're after this book." She held up the book in her hand.

The lawyer's stare was transfixed on the volume. "*The Manor.*" He sighed. "I had heard it was among the items mailed out, but I didn't get to see it, myself."

Jax narrowed his eyes. "Does this book mean something to you?"

The lawyer laughed. "Personally, no. But I believe it's quite valuable. I may be able to find a buyer if you're interested in selling."

"Why is it valuable?"

The lawyer walked around his desk and approached her with a coy smile. "May I?" He held out his hand and Jessa gave him the book. He flipped open to cover. "This in my hand is the only known author-inscribed copy ever found. It's believed he left this note for his lover after he went back to his wife. It's a horrible story. One that's echoed in *The Manor's* pages."

He closed the book and returned it to her. "You're a very lucky woman Ms. Cortez."

"You can see why we're anxious to learn who

might be interested in this book," said Jax.

"The whole world is interested, I imagine," said the lawyer.

Jax nodded. "I need to know who the primary heir of Harold Hopewell's estate is."

The lawyer returned to his seat and opened his folder once more. He appeared to be reading, then lifted his head. "Mr. Hopewell left a series of odd bequests. Single items or amounts of money left to people he was unrelated to. I can only assume that you, Maria Elena, are also one of those people. Is that correct?"

"Yes," she said.

"But he was not without family of his own. He had one sister who passed before him, and she had a son. Harold's only living relative, a nephew. He's the primary heir of Harold's estate. Any of Mr. Hopewell's bequests that go unclaimed will eventually become the property of his nephew."

"I need a name," said Jax.

"I'm sorry, Mr. Andersson. But that's as much as I can help you."

CHAPTER 17

JESSA UP STRAIGHT and squeezed her knees together on the bench seat of Jax's truck. "I want to go back to the beach."

"You're not safe there," said Jax.

"Why not? The guy who was following me is dead. He can't hurt me anymore."

"If he was the only one following you."

"Oh, come on, Jax. You can't just make things up to get me to do what you want."

"I'm not making anything up. I have a hunch the man in the woods was a professional hit man, in which case the person who hired him is still very much alive."

She narrowed her eyes. "What makes you think that?"

"Several things. His rifle. It was a military-issue sniper rifle. You can't walk into a sporting goods store and buy a gun like that. And the GPS unit we found in your purse was also a professional gadget. Do you think the heir of a wealthy millionaire would just happen to have those things, or is he more likely to hire someone who does?"

Jessa turned and stared back out the windshield. "If you're right, I'll never be safe."

"Not as Maria Elena, no."

"I need to get my things, at least."

"Not right now, you don't."

"The only things I care about are in that house."

"They're things, Jessa. They can be replaced."

She knew he was right, though it was the handful of keepsakes she was most concerned with. "Not the special things."

"Then I promise, I'll get them back to you. But for now, we need to head back to Georgia."

"I don't have anywhere to live in Georgia anymore."

"You can stay with me."

She blew out air. She would sooner live on the streets than with this man. "No, thank you."

In that moment, she felt hopeless. All she wanted to do was to create a life for herself and her child where Jax would never find them, and all her attempts to distance herself from him had brought her right back to his side.

"Jessa, I need to know what you were running

from. Why you changed your name. You can trust me with anything."

"Not anything."

"Yes, damn it, anything. But you don't believe that, do you? No matter what I say, you just tune it right out. I'm sorry you feel so alone, but it seems to me you're alone because you don't let anyone inside anymore. I'm your friend, and I'm sitting right here, trying to help, and you're pushing me away as hard as you can."

Her bottom lip was quivering and she bit it, hard. "I want a fresh start, Jax. Away from my memories of Ralph. Away from HERO Force. Away from you."

The truck crested a hill and a gas station came into view. "I need to get fuel," he said. "Are you hungry?"

She nodded, feeling suddenly exhausted, whether from the argument with Jax, the stress of the last few days, or the pregnancy, she had no idea. Probably a bit of everything.

Jax sat in the car and watched Jessa through the gas station window while he touched base with Logan back at HERO Force. "I need everything you've got on this nephew guy," he said. "Somehow he has to be the one orchestrating this shit. No one else has a stake in the items from that will."

"I cross-referenced Hopewell with Maria Elena Cortez. I can't find their association."

"Figures." Jax sighed. "There's one more thing,

Logan, and I need to keep this one under wraps. Even from the other guys."

"Of course."

Jax pursed his lips. Trusting Logan with his deepest concerns was like handing over the keys to the Porsche to a kid without a license. "I need you to find out everything you can about Jessa McConnell, widow of Ralph McConnell."

There was a pause on the line, so that Jax knew Logan was familiar with the name. "Yes, that Ralph. The one from HERO Force."

"What am I looking for?"

Jax leaned his head back against the headrest. That was the twenty-thousand-dollar question. What the hell were they looking for? Something so terrible Jessa would run away from her life. "Anything extreme. She paid money for a new identity, and I want to know why."

"You've got it."

"Thanks, Logan."

Jessa walked toward the car carrying two chocolate milks and two packs of peanut butter cups. She climbed in beside him and handed him one of each.

"Thanks for cooking dinner," he said.

"You're welcome. How long are you planning on driving tonight?"

"Four or five hours."

"Wake me up when we get there." She ate her

peanut butter cups and curled up on her side, facing the window.

Jax drove along the interstate, thinking. He liked having her next to him in his truck, and he didn't like anybody in his truck.

Just like my life.

He liked having her in it, even though she clearly didn't want to be here. They'd be spending tonight at another hotel, then they'd be back in Georgia tomorrow. No doubt she'd exit his life at the first opportunity once they were home.

Unless he could convince her to stay between now and tomorrow afternoon.

Several hours into the drive, his phone rang on the Bluetooth in his ear.

"What did you find out?" he asked Logan.

"She quit her job in Atlanta with notice months before—she clearly planned on moving. She relocated to Savannah, where she'd lined up a nursing job, but for some reason she didn't stay there long. There's only one thing that stands out as strange, but I don't know that it's a reason to take on a new identity. She's been seeing an oncologist, even going so far as to drive back to Atlanta for the appointments."

The lights on the road seemed to blur and drag into streaks of color. "A cancer doctor?"

"That's right. Specializing in ovarian cancer. First, Jessa saw her every few months. Lately, it's been every few weeks."

Jax felt like he was looking at a fun-house mirror where his entire perception of reality had changed in the blink of an eye. He forced his voice past the spasm of his throat. "Anything else?"

"That's all I've got right now."

"Call me the moment you have more information." He disconnected the call.

Jax was a man who wore his armor proudly. He'd worked long and hard to keep his emotions separated from his interactions with the world. But this? His armor was useless against this.

He wanted to punch something, and his hand jabbed at the steering wheel of its own accord. If Jessa were not sleeping next to him, he didn't know what he might do. But she was, and he didn't want to wake her, didn't want to ask her the questions he knew he must ask.

Didn't want to hear those answers.

He drove by a mile-marker sign. The next exit was as good a place as any to stop for the night. He needed a drink.

He needed to explode.

The dotted line down the center of the road flashed like a metronome keeping time in the background. What must she be going through? And a better question yet was how long would he have to wait to find out what was wrong with her?

By the time he pulled into the hotel parking lot, he had himself more under control. At least on the outside. He woke her gently and checked in, again finding only one room with a king-sized bed. Just as she had the last time, Jessa almost immediately took a bath, leaving him by himself.

Ovarian cancer.

He was stunned. Still in shock. He pressed a hand to his stomach, his ulcer burning once more.

He thought back to Jessa in bed, not worried about protection. He remembered when she was carsick and not feeling well. How she didn't drink her coffee. Her dream about having another child. She was sick, possibly very sick, and he was sick not knowing what he might do without her.

Did she know she didn't have to go through this alone? Did she know he would be by her side in a heartbeat, and all she had to do was ask that he be there?

Of course not. How the hell would she know that? They'd spent one night together, and here he was wishing she would tell him what was inside her heart.

She came out of the bathroom and he sat up. "Hey."

"Hey, yourself." She eyed him warily. "Why are you staring at me?"

"Logan called while you were sleeping in the truck." He took a deep breath and let it out slowly. "I know you've been seeing an oncologist."

She turned on him so quickly he jerked his head back in surprise. "How dare you investigate me?"

He stood up. "There has to be a reason. There has to be a reason why you would do all this, why you would leave everything you knew and take on a new identity. It doesn't make any sense, Jessa. I asked you about it, and you didn't tell me the truth. What the hell was I supposed to do?"

She crossed to him. "You know what you don't do? You don't send your dogs digging through my personal life to make yourself feel better. You don't violate my privacy as if you are some god who has the right." She poked her finger into his chest. "You don't do that to someone, Jax. You don't do that to me."

"I'm sorry, Jessa."

"Dr. Davis is an oncologist. She is also my personal physician. Not because I have cancer but because she's my friend. We worked together at the hospital."

Jax bent at the waist. She wasn't sick, wasn't dying. Relief was like a physical loosening of his entire body. "Jesus. You scared the hell out of me."

"Why? What does it matter to you?"

He stood up straight. "I care about you, Jessa. Is that so hard to understand? I see you struggling and I want to help."

"And I don't want your help."

"So you keep telling me. But that doesn't change

anything."

She looked at him like he was crazy. "What the hell is wrong with you, Jax? It was one night. It didn't mean anything to either one of us."

He took a step toward her. "That's not true."

She crossed her arms in front of her chest. "It was one night of bad, lonely sex between two people who ought to know better."

God, she was pushing his buttons. "It meant something to me, and you're lying. It wasn't bad at all." His heart was racing, his will not equipped to stop him from doing what he was about to do. "It was incredible. Maybe I need to jog your memory."

He needed to kiss her, needed to feel her against him after believing for even an instant she might be ill. He couldn't lose her, not to cancer, not to her own belligerence or her insistence she couldn't trust him in her life.

He needed to kiss her, and nothing was going to stand in his way.

CHAPTER 18

S HE INSTANTLY KNEW she had made a mistake.

He moved in and kissed her like he had every right to be kissing her, his lips at once firm and soft and demanding everything she didn't want to give him.

A searing jolt of pure want shot through her body from the point where their mouths connected to the aching emptiness between her legs. She was helpless to control her reaction to this man, no matter how much she disliked him or how angry she had become. She'd seen more emotion from him in the last two days than in all the time she'd known him, and this side of Jax was much more difficult to ignore.

His lips came off of hers, a hair's breadth separating her from him, the sound of their breathing the only sound in her ears. "Tell me you remember," he said, nudging her forehead back with his own and taking her mouth again.

His arms came up around her sides, clenching the fabric at her back. He ground out against her mouth, "Tell me you remember how good it was between us, because I can't stop thinking about it."

She remembered everything.

Every touch, every noise, the rise and fall of their bodies together in the darkness. How she'd tried to make herself forget, willing the memories away as she justified her reaction to him.

She met his eyes, the gleam of knowing satisfaction in his, and she fought against the truth that her body was singing aloud, fought herself to keep her hands from his body. "No," she whispered.

He pulled her against him roughly. "You are such a goddamn liar." He kissed her again, this time his mouth crushing hers, forcing her lips to open and take him inside. Then she was kissing him back, her hands snaking up to wrap around his neck and hold him tightly against her.

He felt so good, better even than that first night, if that was possible. Her body knew now what he could do for her, knew the fireworks they were capable of setting off, and her physical need for him was out of control. She wanted to feel that again. Needed to feel that connection to him.

He pushed her against the wall and growled against her mouth. "Tell me you remember what it felt like when I was inside you, when the whole world stopped moving until I made you come."

He was kissing her neck and she was caught in a landslide, the earth pushing past her while she held on for dear life. "I remember," she whispered. "I remember it all."

He spun her around. Her legs hit the mattress and he followed her down, bracing himself above her as she opened her legs and took the weight of his lower body.

He was lifting her shirt up to her neck, pulling the cups of her bra down to expose her fully.

Would he notice the changes in her body, the fullness of her breasts, how sensitive she'd become?

"The light," she said. "Please turn the light off."

He took one peak into his mouth and sucked deeply.

She yelped in surprised pain.

He let go. "Are you okay?"

She nodded.

"I thought you liked that."

Embarrassment was like ice in a hot drink, instantly cooling her down. She pulled her shirt down between them. "This was a mistake," she said, pushing him off of her, and lowered her legs to the floor.

"Wait…"

She held out her arm to keep him away, suddenly fighting back tears. "No. We're not going to do this again."

His steely stare stayed on her. "Why not?"

"Because I don't want to."

"You're lying."

"No, I'm not. I don't want a fuck buddy in my dead husband's best friend."

"Don't play that card, Jessa. What's between us has nothing to do with him."

She wasn't playing cards, she was grasping at straws. But the conversation was so ingrained in her memory, it was easy to pull out this particular straw. "You may have moved on with your life and forgotten Ralph, but I haven't. I can't. I don't want to. And I can't even look at you without seeing him."

"Bullshit. You didn't think of him at all when we were together. That's why you feel guilty as hell. There were only two of us in that bed, Jessa. Not three, or I damn sure would have noticed. And it kills you that you forgot all about him because you only wanted me."

The truth in his words was like the thinnest of daggers slicing quickly through muscle and digging solidly into bone.

"I hate you," she snarled.

"Maybe you always wanted me, even when you were with him. Maybe that's why you feel so bad."

She reached up to slap him across the face, but he caught her wrist in midair. "Or maybe you didn't. All I know is I was jealous as fuck of that man," he said, "coming home to your warm bed after a mission."

"I'll never forgive you for taking him from me."

He stared at her long and hard, then let go of her wrist. "I'm going to the bar," he said, then turned and was gone.

Jessa stared at the door as the tears came, great gasping sobs for everything she'd done, everything she'd lost, and what she'd been about to do.

God help me.

She had to get out of here. She'd come with Jax because she was in danger, but their stalker was dead now and she no longer had to worry about her safety. It was time to get away from Jax, once and for all.

CHAPTER 19

J AX SAT AT the bar and drank whiskey.

Jessa's words were swirling through his mind as the alcohol swirled in his stomach.

I'll never forgive you for taking him from me.

He took another sip of his drink, but it didn't erase the taste of her from his mouth or wipe clean his memory of her reaction to him. He'd been torturing himself, wondering if everything he remembered about their night together had been exaggerated. Now he was tortured by the fact that it had not.

Yet she hated him.

He'd laid it all on the line, told her how much that night had meant to him, how much he wanted to repeat it, and all she wanted was to forget.

What the hell was he supposed to do with that?

His cell phone rang and he saw it was Logan.

"What's up?"

"I was able to access Jessa's medical records directly."

Jax's stomach clenched. "Go on."

"It's good news. There is nothing about cancer in these files," said Logan. "These records are just for basic checkups, as if she were seeing a general physician."

Relief flooded through Jax. She'd been telling the truth, and he couldn't have been more grateful. Jessa did not have cancer. She was going to be okay.

Thank God.

"Except for one thing," said Logan. "I don't know if it's relevant or not, but since you asked me to look in her files, it seems like maybe it's something I should—"

"What is it, Logan?"

"She's pregnant."

Jax slammed his drink down on the bar. "*What?*"

"Pregnant. You know, she's having a baby."

"I know what the hell pregnant means, you idiot. When is she due?"

"Uh, let me see… looks like March eighteenth."

Jax rolled his eyes. "That was three months ago, Logan."

"Oh no, wait. Sorry. That's the date of her last period. What was that, like two and a half months ago?"

Jax's senses reeled as his mind flew through the

calendar. He needed to get off this phone. Needed to get out of this bar. Somehow he managed to make his voice work. "Anything else?"

"That's all I found."

"Okay, thanks." Jax ended the call with shaking fingers and got to his feet. Any alcoholic haze he'd managed to attain had already evaporated from his mind. He threw money on the bar, not waiting for change, and headed back upstairs to the room.

A baby.

He was going to be a father.

It didn't matter how it happened, didn't matter they hadn't intended to create a new life. He was going to be a father, and Jessa was the mother of his child.

Awe spread its wings wide inside his spirit and he smiled a wobbling smile.

Why hadn't she told him? Didn't she know he'd be happy?

He walked down the corridor, not feeling the floor beneath his feet. In the blink of an eye, his life had changed. He was having a baby with Jessa.

Jesus.

He laughed an awkward laugh that sounded a bit like a sob as he waited for the elevator. He was going to be a father.

He reached their hotel room and inserted his key. She stood beside the bed and straightened when he walked in. He let his eyes feast on her face. What would their child look like? Would he have her black hair, the sharpened features of her Cherokee face?

"Why didn't you tell me?" he asked.

"What?"

His eyes dropped from hers and took in her breasts, her belly, and back up again. He remembered how she'd flinched in pain when he suckled her breast. How she'd ignored the coffee and wine he'd bought for her. Her apparent sickness in the truck. He felt for what she was already going through, the changes that were taking place in her body. "About the baby."

Her eyes went wide and her mouth opened.

"Logan got your medical records. I know you're pregnant." His lips pressed together as he smiled. "I know you're carrying my child." He walked toward her and opened his arms.

She pushed him away. "You had no right to go through my medical records!"

"I was worried about you. We can do this, Jessa. Everything will be okay. I'll support you and the baby. We'll raise the baby together—"

"No! You had no right to go through my medical records. You just think you can do anything, that nobody's in charge of you. And you don't care who gets hurt in the process."

"I needed to know why you bought a new identity, what you're running away from. We've been looking at everything. Financial, medical. I need to understand why you ran away, and you weren't helping me…"

A horrible understanding polarized his brain, and for a long moment he simply stared at her while the pieces slipped quietly into place. "Wait a second." He ran a hand through his hair. "You knew you were pregnant and you didn't tell me. You weren't going to tell me."

The look on her face was full of such hatred he was taken aback.

"Oh my God," he whispered. "You were running from me."

She took a step backwards and he advanced on her. "You were running from me!" He shook his head, disbelief attempting to derail what was clearly the truth. "You were running from me so I wouldn't know about the baby!"

No visitation.

Anger burst forth from him like hot lava into the sky. He turned and smashed his fist through the wall, pleased when Jessa jumped.

"My baby," she whispered.

"Ours!" he yelled. "You weren't going to tell me. You're carrying my child, and you weren't even going to fucking tell me! That's why you wanted a new identity, so I couldn't find you. So I couldn't find you and my own child."

Her stare was icy.

"It must have been horrible for you," he said.

"Getting pregnant by the one man you can't stand."

"An eye for an eye."

"*What did you say?*"

"I lost my baby when you killed Ralph. You owed me one."

He put one hand on either side of his head and turned away from her and this craziness. Not even Linda's betrayals compared to this. That's when he saw her bag packed and ready to go. He pointed to it and turned back to her. "If I hadn't come back just now, you would have been gone."

She crossed her arms.

He stormed to her. "Answer me! If I hadn't come back here, would you have left?"

She glared at him and spit out between her teeth, "Hell yes, I would have left. I can't stand you. I don't want you in my life or my baby's life."

"Well then, we're just going to have to make sure you stick around." He dug in his bag and withdrew a pair of handcuffs. He turned to her, pleased when a knowing look appeared in her eyes.

"No."

"You don't get to decide anymore." He put one handcuff around her wrist and the other around the arm of a heavy chair. "And you sure as hell don't get to walk out of here with my child."

All he could see in his mind's eye was Jessa, beautiful Jessa, naked beneath him and guiding him inside her without a condom.

I want you to come inside me.

She'd been planning to steal from him, to take the one thing more precious than any other. The family that rightfully belonged to him.

CHAPTER 20

J ESSA WEPT INTO her pillow in the darkened hotel room. When it was time for sleep, Jax had chained her to the bed frame using the handcuffs and some cable he had in the car. Now he lay beside her, sleeping as she cried.

She touched her lower abdomen.

I'm so sorry, baby.

She'd been a fool to think she could get away from Jax, to have thought she could keep the child a secret forever. She remembered Jax's face as he accused her of everything she had done. There was some comfort in the hatred she saw there. At least it was better than the wanting.

She had no defense against that.

She squeezed her eyes shut and a fresh crop of tears made their way to the pillow. Her baby was the one who was going to pay the price for this. Her baby was the one who would be stuck with a tin man for a father. It wasn't fair, but nothing was ever fair.

Ralph was the one who should have been her child's father, Ralph was the one who wanted a baby with her, who would have been such an incredible dad.

Not Jax.

Never Jax.

She thought of Linda, Jax's ex-wife, back in the day when Linda and Jax were still married. The two women had been friends, if not the best of friends. They had a lot in common back then, each of them married to a man who was married to HERO Force. Linda had told Jessa how cold Jax could be. How unforgiving. He'd made Linda's life miserable, and now he was going to make her and her child's life miserable as well.

It's all my fault.

She took a shaking breath in and felt the mattress move as Jax rolled over. He was invading her personal space by sharing the bed with her, but he told her chivalry died the moment she decided to take his son or daughter away. So here she was, tethered to a bed in a motel room with the one man who she desperately wanted to get away from.

What the hell was she going to do?

She needed a plan. Something to work for. If only he would realize what a terrible father he would make, how much better off this baby would be without him, then surely he would not choose to be a part of its life.

Would he?

Ralph used to say Jax was tenacious as a pit bull. She clearly remembered how brutally Jax had ripped apart his ex-wife in court. She and Ralph had even fought about it—her defending Linda, him clearly on Jax's side. She'd made a fool out of him, Ralph said, and broken his heart. Jessa was fairly certain Jax didn't have a heart, and personally held Linda blameless.

At least Linda had managed to get away from Jax, while here she was, sharing a bed with him.

And let's not forget, you're carrying his child.

Her baby. Not his.

Hers.

CHAPTER 21

JAX STARED UNSEEING into the room. The bed trembled as he listened to Jessa cry. Not that he had a lot of sympathy for her. She deserved anything that came her way after what she had done to him. He still couldn't believe it. Sweet Jessa, who'd never hurt anyone in her life as far as he knew, had planned and schemed to take keep his child from him.

Was there anything worse in the world?

His eyes closed of their own volition.

I want you to come inside me, Jax.

God, how those words had turned him on. He'd wanted to lay claim to her, to have his body mix inside her—hell, yes, maybe have the potential to change everything. He sighed. Not that he knew she was going to get pregnant, of course not. But in that moment, if she had told him she wanted a baby, he would happily have obliged.

Not if you knew she intended to cut you out of that child's life forever.

He hadn't given her hatred enough credit, hadn't realized how truly and completely she had wished him ill. He'd known she was angry, sure. He'd known she was hurt, grieving, even. But he had not understood the lengths to which she would go to get back at him.

So what the hell was he going to do now? He wanted her to have the baby. There was no question about that. That little boy or girl was so tiny right now, but already he loved it. That was the hardest part. Because right now, he could not see a way that this would work out as a happy family for his child.

Whether the baby ended up with Jessa alone or with him alone or with some awkward and hellish arrangement in between, he couldn't see a happy life emerging from this mess.

A child of his deserved better than that.

He rolled over and looked at the ceiling, staring at the shadows there as if they might hold the answers to the universe's major questions.

A baby.

God, it was hard to believe. He'd wanted to be a father for as long as he could remember. Now somewhere inside Jessa was a tiny human being made of her and him.

He smiled in the darkness.

He had to find a way for this child to have a good life. And, much as he didn't want to admit it, the baby's best chance for happiness depended on his own ability to live with the child's mother.

I may never be able to do that.

He wanted to kill her.

He looked over at the silhouette of her body outlined by the covers. Just yesterday, he'd been fighting for her life. Willing to lay down his own if it meant she would be okay.

Thank God that was over. Yes, the rotten liar was safe, and he would do whatever he had to do to make sure she stayed that way. But live with her? Trust her and let her get close to him?

No way.

CHAPTER 22

"WHERE ARE WE going?" asked Jessa.

They'd already been driving for almost an hour, and she hadn't even bothered to ask. Jax was clearly in a foul mood—not that she could blame him—and she had little desire to incur his wrath once again.

"I'm taking you to my house."

She had suspected as much. She didn't have a house to go to, and he clearly wasn't planning on letting her out of his sight. She was weak from being in his presence, from the lies and the emotional uproar of him finding out she was pregnant. No, she was tired of him before that. Needing her space. "And then what? You can't keep me handcuffed forever."

He shot her a wry look. "Why not?"

Jessa shook her head and looked out the window.

"Sooner or later, you're going to have to let me go. You do know that, so why are you pretending?"

"I'm not pretending anything, Jessa. I'll leave that to you. I would just like to know that you're not going to run off with my kid the minute I turn my back. And until I feel comfortable that isn't going to happen, you're going to stay tied up like a Doberman."

She scoffed. "Just slightly illegal."

"It's a hell of a lot better than what you did to me, honey."

They drove the rest of the distance in silence, all of Jessa's plans to convince him he'd be a lousy parent falling by the wayside. She couldn't talk to him when he was like this. There was no point. He was as stubborn as hell, and there wasn't a damn thing she could do about that.

She vaguely recognized the mountain he lived on when they got to it, the twisting and turning road bringing her nausea back to life. The last time she'd been here had been with Ralph. "I think I'm going to be sick."

"Just pretend I don't know you're pregnant. That ought to settle your stomach right down."

She glared at him. "This is not a joke, Jax. I've had morning sickness for weeks now."

"Forgive me if I'm running low on sympathy for you at the moment."

"Forget it. Just forget it."

Jax slowed to a crawl near a tall wrought iron gate. He frowned.

"What's wrong?" she asked.

"Someone's been here." He pointed to a set of tire tracks faintly visible in the wet leaves to the side of the gate. "I wasn't expecting any visitors." He reached over her lap to open the glove compartment and retrieved his weapon, noting how she shied away from him as he did.

"Do you always reach for a gun when you have a houseguest?" she asked.

Jax stared at her. "This is not a houseguest, Jessa. The only houseguests that I get know damn well not to drive around the security gate. I'm wondering if this might be a special visit courtesy of that fancy lawyer in Boston."

He could see his words register on her sense of security, her eyes widening with concern.

"What do you mean?" she asked. "We already killed the man who was after me."

"He may not be the only one. If he was paid to go after you, then the person who hired him might have hired someone in his place."

She closed her eyes and pressed a hand to her stomach. "Why only one? Why not send two?"

"Or three, or four."

Her eyes popped open.

"We don't know what we're dealing with here,

Jessa. For all we know, that lawyer tipped someone off that Maria Elena was there looking for answers. And that she wasn't alone."

Jessa's eyes widened. "Oh my God, did we give them your name?"

He nodded once. "I did. Do you want to know how many Jax Andersson's there are in the United States?"

She took a deep breath in and exhaled slowly. "No, I don't think I do."

Jax hit a button on the dashboard of his car, and the gates opened wide. "There are three." They drove up to the house without talking, a sprawling cedar two-story that settled into the mountainside like a cliff.

Jessa's first visit here had been when Jax and Linda were still married, for a skiing weekend with Ralph. She remembered being impressed by the sprawling house, with its cedar siding, tall windows, and rambling floor plan. It was mere weeks before Jax announced he and Linda were splitting up, and the couple was clearly not getting along.

The weekend from hell.

One evening in particular, Jessa had overheard the pair arguing in the kitchen late at night when she'd gone to get a glass of water. She should have walked away when she heard Linda say, "You don't even touch me anymore," but her curiosity had gotten the better of her.

Jax's voice had been deep and filled with pain. "I

touch your skin, and I wonder who's touched you there before me. I wonder when."

"We have to move forward, Jax. We can't keep dwelling in the past."

"I wonder if you brought them into our bed." The sound of a chair squeaking across the floor. "Did you, Linda? Did you bring them into our bed? Did you tell them how lonely it is with your husband gone for weeks at a time?"

"Stop it."

"Christ, you did, didn't you? You let them fuck you right there. What else did you do?"

"I was lonely, Jax! All the time. Even when you were right next to me, I was lonely. I still am. You shut me out with a single look, and damned if I know how to get back in."

"Then I'll go grab your cell phone and you can make a booty call to one of the guys you've been fucking. Maybe barebacking on the living room sofa we picked out together will help you sleep."

He'd rounded the corner to the stairs, nearly colliding with Jessa.

She'd been horrified.

It hadn't even occurred to her that Jax might still live in the same house.

Jax opened the garage door but did not pull inside. He turned to her. "I want you to wait here." He looked at her handcuffs, clearly considering, then cursed under his breath before unlocking them. "Never mind, you're coming with me."

"But…"

"But nothing. I can't leave you here handcuffed. You won't be able to defend yourself. And I can't give you the keys because we both know you'd be gone faster than a bat out of hell. Which leaves us with only one option."

He walked into the garage and opened a storage locker, withdrawing a dark vest. He brought it back to her. "Put this on." He handed her a weapon. "I'm just going to have to trust you don't hate me enough to kill me."

With that, he led the way inside. "We're going to clear each room, one by one. You stay behind me, never in front, or I might shoot you."

She slipped her arms into the bulletproof vest. "Seems we'll just have to trust each other, then."

CHAPTER 23

J AX WATCHED AS Jessa pushed her pasta around her plate with a fork. She'd hardly eaten anything, and he wondered if that was her new normal now that she was pregnant. "Is there something else I can get you to eat?"

She put her fork down. "No, it's just not sitting very well."

He nodded, picking up her plate and taking it to the sink.

They'd gone through the house room by room finding no one and nothing visibly disturbed, then checked the logs from the security system. Nothing seemed out of place, no sensors on the house alerted in his absence, but Jax remained convinced someone had been there. Hell, they might still be outside. The woods around this house could provide cover for the masses.

He needed to upgrade his security system. Install video surveillance at the gate and around the perimeter of the property.

"So," said Jessa, "I've been thinking. About you and me and the baby... What it's going to be like."

He rinsed her pasta into the garbage disposal. "Go on, I'm listening."

"I know you never wanted kids. That doesn't have to change."

He turned around and leaned back against the counter. "When were you discussing my life goals? With Linda?"

She nodded. "We were friends."

"Yes, I remember. Maybe I should explain a few things to you about my ex-wife."

Jessa held up her hands. "Whatever happened between the two of you is none of my business."

"Before today, I would have agreed with you. Now I think it's important you understand what really happened. She cheated on me, nearly every time we went wheels up. Lots of different men, lots of different times. Did you know that?"

"I overheard you guys arguing that night."

"That's right. You did."

"I remember she was very lonely."

"She was a goddamn liar, that's what she was. Seems you two have something in common there."

Jessa narrowed her eyes at him.

Jax shrugged. "Besides sharing my bed, that is." He watched as her face flushed with anger, momentarily pleased he was the one who put it there. He wanted her to be angry. He wanted her to be hurt. He wanted her to feel even a fraction of the hell she was putting him through now.

"You know what I keep thinking?" asked Jessa. "That some people just aren't meant to have children. They're not nurturing, they're not warm. Just because I'm pregnant, Jax, doesn't mean you have to be a father."

He walked around behind her chair and put his hands on her shoulders. "If you wanted an absentee father for your kid, you should have run faster." He squeezed her shoulders, enjoying how she shook him off.

"I've been doing some thinking of my own," he said. "And I thought maybe I should have primary custody, and you should be the one to get visitation."

She shot out of her chair. "No!"

"I mean, it seems only fair. You decided to bring this new life into the world. I should get to decide what we do with it."

"You will make a terrible father. The only emotion you know how to show is anger."

He froze. All his life he'd been told he was cold, unemotional, but none of those comments ever hurt quite like this one. "Could be worse," he said. "I could have forgotten how to smile." He watched as her face fell, his comment hitting home. The volley of insults reminded him of his ex-wife. "I think we've talked enough for tonight. It's time for us to get some sleep."

She crossed her arms. "I'm not sleeping next to you again."

He had expected as much. Fortunately, he already had another plan. "No, you'll be sleeping in the guest room. Second door on the left. There are clean clothes for you on the bed."

He watched her go, noting the curious look she gave him at the apparent reprieve from his watchful stare this evening, then finished straightening the kitchen while her words echoed in his head.

You will make a terrible father.

The only emotion you know how to show is anger.

She was good at locating his Achilles heel, that much was sure. He walked up the stairs, stopping in an empty room Linda had used for crafts. It was supposed to be a child's room, but that child had never come. In the end he knew why—his wife had secretly been on birth control throughout their marriage.

What a fool he'd been.

Now Jessa was carrying his child and she didn't want him in the baby's life. Not that she would win that battle, of course, but her accusations touched on the major concern he had about fatherhood—that he wouldn't be affectionate enough with the child.

He walked to the window. She should be dressed by now and enjoying her newfound freedom, if not already planning her escape. He walked to his bedroom and opened the nightstand drawer, a smile lighting his features as he pictured what she had in store.

CHAPTER 24

JESSA CHANGED INTO the large T-shirt he left for her, grateful for the clean clothes after her shower, and made her way back to the guest room. The bed was big and tall and fluffy, covered in a white comforter and lots of pillows. She sighed, relieved she would finally get to spend the night by herself, and climbed under the covers.

Jax knocked once and opened the door. "All set for bed?"

"For the love of God, just lock me in here and leave me alone."

He clucked his tongue. "Sorry, sweetheart, there's no lock on the door. But I brought something for you."

She eyed him warily. "What is that?"

He moved to the end of the bed and sat down, pulling the blankets out to expose her feet, and her stomach clenched.

"What are you doing?" she asked.

His voice was husky. "Just making sure you're here in the morning."

He picked up her foot and wrapped something soft around her ankle. She pushed down the puffy blanket so she could see what he had placed there—a black velvet cuff with red rope running from it.

A sex toy.

She gasped. "You can't be serious…"

"Oh, I'm serious all right. You tried to take my child out of my life. I'll do whatever I have to do to keep you here." He raised one eyebrow. "I think you'll find they're pretty comfortable."

"Just a little something you happened to have lying around?"

He shrugged. "They're made for holding someone against a bed. They seemed appropriate."

He reached for her other foot and she snatched it away. "Would you rather sleep in my bed tonight?" he asked. His eyes were dark, and they held a silent threat that clearly told her the sex toy was the least dangerous option.

She pursed her lips. "How am I supposed to move?"

"I'll leave enough play in the lines. As long as you can't reach the other straps to unfasten them, that's all I care about."

She glared at him, then slowly put her leg back within his reach. He touched her and her leg jerked as he placed the band around her ankle and secured it tightly.

She couldn't help but wonder what woman he'd tied to his bed before her. Was that how he liked it, with one partner immobile?

Or maybe the tie-downs are for him.

An image of Jax naked and spread eagle on the bed emerged unbidden in her mind. His glorious muscles. His cock erect and full.

Lord have mercy.

But who was the woman who would straddle him?

She watched as he tucked a length of red rope under the mattress, then moved to the side of the bed and pulled it back out. She licked her lips.

"Give me your hand," he said.

She was beginning to feel way too vulnerable, and she was shaking. "This is ridiculous."

"All right, then." He pulled back the covers, exposing her body and bare legs. "I'll sleep in here with you."

"Whoa, wait, stop!" She grabbed the blankets and pulled them back up with a huff. "Fine. Tie me up, but you're not sleeping here." She glared at him as his too-warm fingers wrapped around her wrist and pulled it toward him, then fastened the velvet strap securely.

He walked to the opposite side of the bed, trailing

the red rope up the underside of the mattress as he went. He sat down on the edge of the bed and held out his hand expectantly.

Her heart was racing. As soon as she gave him her hand, he would have all four of her limbs secured.

"Give me your hand, Jessa."

She took a deep breath in and out, imploring him with her eyes not to make her do this.

"I'm not going to hurt you," he said, but there was a change in him, a dangerous fierceness to his voice that made her feel like she was a bunny looking for comfort from a fox.

She closed her eyes and held out her hand.

His fingers closed around her more tightly this time, his hand lightly caressing hers before he secured the velvet strap, but he didn't release her.

Jessa held her breath.

It must be the pregnancy hormones, because she was overwhelmed with intense physical longing, the connection between them seeming to magnify every sensation as he stroked her fiery skin.

She opened her eyes, her lids heavy with desire, and saw an answering arousal on his face that frightened her to her core. This was the man she professed to hate, the father of her child, a man truly worthy of the horrible betrayal she'd bestowed upon him.

So why am I attracted to him?

He stared at her for what seemed a long time, the

tension between them stretching out like the bands that held her to the bed. Then the pressure of his hands on her changed, pulling him toward her. "Damn you," he growled.

He leaned in and kissed her, his mouth demanding and rough. She pulled at her restraints, her arms reaching for him, though whether to hold on to him tightly or push him away, she wasn't sure. But she could do neither, she could only take his kisses as she lay beneath him, open and exposed.

Her mind might have been confused, but her body was not, its will made known by the twist of her hips against the mattress and the subtle moans of pleasure coming from deep in her throat.

Jax's hand came up to her breast and squeezed, shocking her sensitive peak and making her arch her back as she gasped. He deepened the kiss, the hard bridge of his erection grinding into her hip, and she pushed back against him suggestively.

She was vaguely aware of the insanity in her movements and the hot flush of arousal covering her body. She hated him so much, yet that emotion did nothing to douse the flames of desire that flared up when he was near. On the contrary, it seemed to make him that much more irresistible.

He slid his hands under the T-shirt he'd given her, pushing the fabric up to reveal her to him. He exhaled a shaking breath and took one breast in each hand, forcing her nipples out of the holes made by his thumb and forefinger before lapping at each one with his tongue. She cried out in pleasure. She was wickedly aroused, her body screaming and desperate for him to make love to her again as he'd done that first night, knowing his touch held the magic she craved to be free of her past.

"Please, Jax," she begged.

Their eyes locked, her lids heavy with desire.

His hands fell away from her body, and cool air grazed her skin where he'd held her tightly. "This is crazy," he said.

It was as if the world suddenly stopped spinning, everything falling over as momentum turned into a destructive force. She curled her fingers into her palms and bit her lip, hard.

He looked around the room like he'd just awakened from sleepwalking. He stared at her half-naked body. "What the hell am I doing?"

He pulled her shirt down, the blanket up over her, and got up. He scrubbed his face with his palms before leaving the room, closing the door firmly behind him.

Jessa was alone—just as she'd wanted—a frantic sort of desperation her only companion for the night.

CHAPTER 25

J ESSA AWOKE TO the sound of deep male voices in quiet conversation. When one of them barked with laughter, her eyes popped open.

Cowboy.

She smiled widely and moved to get up, surprised when she realized her hands were bound together with part of the sex bindings from last night and affixed with a tiny padlock.

At least she was no longer attached to the bed. She furrowed her brow, wondering when Jax had made the change.

Cowboy laughed again in the distance. It had been forever since she'd seen him, and forever was much too long to go without seeing a friend like she had in Leo Wilson. He was a ray of sunshine in a world full of raindrops, and she'd missed him terribly.

"Jax, how could you leave me like this?" She looked down at her body. At least she had a shirt on.

She stood and made her way to the top of the stairs. "Jax?" she called down. The men kept talking as if they didn't hear. She sighed and moved down the steps, stopping short of the doorway to the kitchen. "Jax?" she called again.

"That's Jessa," Jax said. "Why don't you go and say hi?"

"Jessa McConnell?" Cowboy came into view at the bottom of the stairs, and Jessa grinned warily. She was barely covered up and wearing a pair of velvet handcuffs. What would he think of her?

She needn't have worried. Cowboy gave a loud whoop and opened his arms to greet her, hopping up two stairs when she wasn't quick enough to leap into his embrace.

"Damn, girl, it's good to see you." He pulled back, his eyes scanning from her head to her waist. "Looking sexy, too." He picked up her hand and furrowed his brow. "What is this?"

"Uh…"

Jax appeared in the doorway, dressed to a T and clearly back in command of his emotions.

And everyone around him.

Her toes curled into the rug.

Jax looked from her to Cowboy and back again. "I see you remember Leo."

He looked angry, and she felt like she'd done something wrong, though she wasn't sure why. "Of course I do."

Jax took a small key out of his pocket and unlocked her wrists.

Cowboy smiled widely. "If I'd known it was that kind of party, I'd have brought my whips and chains."

Jessa was embarrassed, but Jax just laughed good-naturedly, making her wonder if she'd been right about his anger just a moment before.

"You two seeing each other?" Cowboy asked.

Jessa and Jax answered at the same time.

"No," said Jessa.

"We're having a baby," said Jax.

Cowboy's mouth pulled into a disbelieving half grin. "Together?"

Jax pointed at her with his chin. "Tell him, *sweetie.*"

At that very moment, her morning sickness reared its ugly head and she pressed a hand to her stomach.

"Are you okay?" asked Cowboy.

"She's fine," said Jax. "Just happy."

She brought her hand to her mouth and ran for the bathroom, aware and horrified that her ass was hanging out of the back of her shirt. She heard Jax say, "She's glowing. Don't you think?" and she wished he were closer so she could throw up on his perfectly shined shoes.

When she was done being sick, she sat on the

washroom floor and rested her head in her hands.

She thought back over the last six months. The increasing sense that life was passing her by, her determination to get out of the house where her marriage lived like a ghost that was haunting her present.

So, she'd packed up everything she owned and made a new plan—move to Savannah and start fresh. A new hospital, a new town, a new life.

Then Jax showed up at her door.

She cursed and wiped at her eyes.

She'd thought her days with HERO Force were over, that she'd never see any of those guys ever again. But there he was, standing on her doorstep in the bright sunshine, just waiting to take her newfound independence and throw her back in time.

In the blink of an eye, she was stuck again, the sad young widow who had lost her happiness. And she just about lost her mind.

Hell, maybe I did lose it.

She remembered getting ready to go to the bar and find Jax. She remembered her plan, which was now well executed. Seduce him. Get pregnant. Go on with her life a little better than she'd been before, the replacement of a baby in her womb like a pound of flesh that could make everything better.

Only it hadn't made anything better at all.

She loved this baby with all her heart and soul, but

she knew now it could never replace the one she'd lost. That was the baby she and Ralph had created out of love, and it died when he did.

She stood and started the water running, then stripped and stepped into the tub. A stirring like the tickling of butterfly wings in her lower belly made her gasp.

"Baby," she whispered, a smile spreading over her face and a joyous giggle rising up in her throat. "Hi, sweetheart." Then she was crying happy tears, so happy was she to feel her baby move. She didn't know if she'd ever feel that again after her first baby died, and the sensation meant more to her than she could have imagined.

By the time she made it back downstairs, she was determined Jax was not going to ruin her newfound good mood.

"You're sure it was him?" asked Jax.

Cowboy's voice was deep and loud. "Ballistics confirmed the weapon was the same one used in a murder four years ago in Boston. Funny thing is, the defendant's attorney works for Layton, Felder, Bach & Moore. The weapon went missing during the trial."

She walked into the room. "What's going on?"

Jax met her eyes. "It looks like Maria Elena may have been killed by someone from the law firm in Boston."

"Or someone who worked on one of their cases," said Cowboy. "The police. The legal staff. Opposing counsel."

She leaned away from him. "How do you know?"

"Ballistics match from the bullet that killed Maria Elena to the one that was used on an old case handled by the law firm. The alleged shooter was acquitted of all charges."

"That doesn't make any sense," she said. "The lawyers wouldn't want the heir dead. They don't benefit."

"Unless the person connected to the law firm is also Harold's nephew. I'll have Logan look into it," said Jax, opening his cell phone and placing the call.

Cowboy turned to her. "You're a sight for sore eyes, baby cakes. What do you say I take you to lunch?"

Jessa turned to Jax, who didn't seem to notice. "Sure," she said to Cowboy. "I'd like that, if my captor doesn't mind letting me out of my cage for a while."

Jax glared at her and she knew he was listening.

"I already asked him," said Cowboy. "Seems I'm to treat you as an unfriendly and never let you out of my sight." He laughed.

"I wasn't kidding, Cowboy," said Jax.

"Oh, I know it."

Jessa stuck out her bottom lip.

"Still want to go to lunch with me?" Cowboy asked.

She nodded. "Anything to get out of here."

CHAPTER 26

JESSA PICKED AT her salad while Cowboy took a bite of a big, juicy cheeseburger dripping with fried onions. The smell was appalling. Not that she had any appetite lately, anyway.

"I called you a few times," said Cowboy.

"I know." She eyed him sheepishly. "I wasn't ready to talk."

"Jax told me about the baby you lost. I'm real sorry, Jessa."

"Thanks."

"I hate to think you were going through that all by yourself."

Her stomach threatened to reject the minestrone soup she'd just consumed, and she put her spoon down with resolve. "What about you, Leo? There anyone special in your life?"

"Always."

She laughed. "Just one woman?"

He scowled. "Of course not, Jess. Have we met before?" He held out his hand. "I'm Leo Wilson."

"I see."

He picked up his mammoth burger. "What about you? Are you really having a baby with Jax?"

"I'm really having a baby, and Jax is technically the father."

"You couldn't do any better for father material than Jax."

"What do you mean?"

"He's the greatest leader I've ever known, and I've known some. An honest man. I respect him, and I don't respect a whole hell of a lot of people."

He stared at her to the point of making her uncomfortable.

"If you don't mind me asking," he said, "how did you two end up together?"

"We're not together. And just because he's good at killing people and blowing things up doesn't mean he'd be a good father. There's an entirely different set of job requirements for those two positions."

"Are you kidding me?" Cowboy asked. "Maybe you ain't never seen him, but he's great with kids. They run a crack right through that tough-guy exterior to the gushy middle inside. He wanted kids bad when he was married to Linda."

"No, he didn't."

Cowboy turned his head and eyed her from under his brow. "Yeah, he did. But Linda was on birth control and hiding it. You should ask him about it."

Coming from Cowboy, Jessa knew it was true, and she felt a pang of sympathy for Jax and his relationship with Linda. First his wife lied to him about having children, then she'd tried to take one away.

Don't feel bad for him now!

She conjured an image of Jax in her living room, telling her Steele was dead, and the memory had the desired effect. She remembered why she hated Jax Andersson.

"I don't care what happened between Jax and his ex-wife," she said.

"Seems to me, you ain't caring about the people you need to be caring about right now."

She raised her head. "Excuse me?"

"I'm sure you think you're doing what's best, but you're just watching out for yourself. Being a good mom might be more important to you than anything, but you have to realize you might not be the only person this kid needs in his life."

"Jax has fewer emotions than a robot. What kind of parent will he be?"

"Your kid couldn't do better. And if you don't see that, you ain't looking at things straight on like you ought to."

"He's holding me against my will, Leo. He tied me to the bed so I couldn't leave. That's why he jokingly insisted you not let me out of your sight. It's not a joke at all."

"He doesn't want you to disappear with his son or daughter. Can't say I blame the man for that."

"He told you that."

Cowboy nodded. "He did. Can't say as I believed him at first, but it's true, ain't it?"

She looked at the tablecloth.

"It's hard for me to see two people I care about tear each other apart," he said. "Worst part of it is, I think if the two of you got your heads screwed on straight, you'd realize you're the best thing for each other."

"No way."

"C'mon. I think it's time for me to bring you back to Jax now."

"So he can handcuff me to the bedpost and hold me hostage?"

"If that's what he chooses to do, then yes ma'am."

She stood up, raising her voice in the restaurant. "This is absurd. Inhumane."

Cowboy leaned in close, taking her elbow in his hand. "If you've got any sense left in your mind, you should love that man."

"What?"

"You could do a hell of a lot worse, Jessa."

Over Cowboy's shoulder, she saw Jax walk into the restaurant. Cowboy must have seen from her expression that there was something worth turning around for.

"What is he doing here?" she asked.

"I don't think he trusted me with his prized hostage. I'm going to say goodbye now, kitten," he said, moving forward and planting a kiss on her cheek. "It was good to see you doing so well."

Jessa was left stammering in her old friend's wake as Jax crossed the room. "We need to stop at HERO Force while we're out," he said.

She shook her head quickly. "No. I'm not going back there."

"We have to, Jessa. There are things that need to be done to make sure you stay safe."

She couldn't take much more of this. She was at her breaking point, completely out of the emotional energy it would take to go into that building, but also not prepared for another fight. "Fine. One stop at HERO Force, and I'm done."

CHAPTER 27

THE ELEVATOR SHOT upward and Jessa's stomach lurched. This time her discomfort had nothing to do with morning sickness and a whole lot to do with the building they were in. The Alpha squadron headquarters of HERO Force looked like any old building from the outside, but once they went inside those front doors, it could only be likened to itself, with long governmental hallways, retinal scanners beside every other doorway, and overhead lights that gave everything an omniscient glow.

She hated this building. She had always hated this building.

Cowboy shot her an understanding look, but Jax seemed oblivious to her distress.

She hadn't been here since Ralph was alive, and even then her visits had been infrequent. There was no reason for her to come to HERO Force, and it wasn't a building that was easily accessible for people who weren't part of the team. The elevator came to an abrupt halt, the doors opening to an area lit by a blue security light.

Oh God, I hate this so much.

"Good afternoon, Mr. Andersson. The team is waiting for you in conference room three."

Jax nodded almost imperceptibly. "Thank you."

The receptionist eyed Jessa with obvious curiosity, and Jessa wondered if the other woman remembered she was Ralph's wife or if she was simply shocked to see another woman inside the hallowed walls of this testosterone castle.

Jax bent at the waist and stared into a scanner, the doorway beside it sliding open with a whoosh, and he stepped back for Jessa to enter before him.

Her legs were quaking as she walked, memories flitting through her consciousness. A memory of her husband teased the edge of her mind, Ralph explaining why they were going wheels up just days after returning from a mission.

We have to extract the girl as quickly as possible.

Extract the girl, and easy euphemism for the type of mission she knew well. You couldn't be married to a Navy SEAL for long without understanding extraction was a fancy word for going after the bad guys, guns blazing, your life on the line for someone else's in the dark of night.

The last time there'd been an extraction, Ralph had come home with a shiny new bullet hole in his leg. Jessa might have hated this, but she'd loved the man, and God knew the man loved the job.

They rounded a corner and several desks came into view. A young man stood up and bent his head in recognition. "Mrs. McConnell, it's good to see you again."

"Thank you." Her stomach rolled, and she wished she could vomit. Perhaps then she would feel better, purge herself of this awful feeling that HERO Force instilled in her to this day.

She met the empty stares of the others around him, people she once knew casually who now seemed to see straight through her.

I'm a reminder of everything that could ever go wrong.

Jax stopped walking and turned to her. "Why don't you wait in my office?"

She didn't know where that was, which in and of itself was a reprieve. She nodded.

He lowered his voice. "I'll have someone stationed outside the door."

"In case I try to leave."

"Yes."

She narrowed her eyes. "I wonder what your loyal HERO Force subjects would think if they knew you slept with Ralph's wife?"

His eyes narrowed. "Ralph is gone, Jessa. Dead men don't have wives."

"You son of a bitch." She stole a glance at Cowboy, who had moved several steps away and was pretending he could not hear. "You can be as much of an asshole as you want to be, but don't you ever say that about my husband again."

"What? That he's dead? Or that I shouldn't have to act like he's alive when his widow is carrying my child?"

She reached up and slapped him across the face. For a moment, he registered no reaction at all, then he grabbed her by the elbow and marched several yards down a hallway, pulling her inside a dark room and turning on the lights.

He bit out his words. "You do realize the irony here is that nothing I said is untrue. Ralph is dead and gone. He is no longer married to you, remember? Till death do us part. Now you might miss him, but that does not mean we did anything wrong when we slept together. So don't imply I have something to be ashamed about in front of my coworkers, or even God himself, because I don't—"

"Let me go."

"And you don't, either. Even though you planned all this, and right now you can't forgive yourself for doing it, you did not betray your husband."

She yanked her arm away from him. "I don't need

your absolution."

Jax stared at her, his hard eyes giving nothing away. "Suit yourself." He walked out of the office, closing the door behind him.

CHAPTER 28

J
AX LOOKED AROUND at the members of HERO Force Alpha squadron. "Whoever killed Maria Elena had access to the gun from the trial. We need to find out who that is. We also need to check out the nephew. He inherited the bulk of Harold Hopewell's estate, and near as I can figure, he's the only one with something to gain from Maria Elena's death."

Cowboy leaned forward in his chair. "Find out how the law firm is connected to the nephew, and we'll find our killer."

Red spoke up. "We got a positive ID on the tango you took down, Jax. Albert Volcht, a German nationalist who made his living as a professional hit man."

"I was afraid of that," said Jax. "Who's he work for?"

"More or less, a freelancer. Hasn't had any known

associations in almost twenty years."

"So whoever contracted the hit is still out there."

Red nodded. "Looks that way."

Jax's mind was racing. "There was someone in my house. Two, maybe three days ago. They went around the security gate. Nothing was amiss inside. I want upgrades to the security system at my house, starting with a secure perimeter and cameras all around."

He looked to Matteo. "Red, take Hawk and some of the guys from tech and take care of it. As long as Jessa's staying with me, I need to know when someone's there."

"All due respect, Jax, what if there's trouble?" asked Cowboy. "You're too far in the boondocks for anyone to get there in a reasonable amount of time."

Jax ran his hand over a thick scar on his chin. Normally he was confident in his ability to protect himself. But this was Jessa's security they were talking about—Jessa and his child—and that changed things.

That changed things a lot.

He nodded. "Cowboy, you and Logan set up in the bunkhouse until we're through with this mess."

Logan sat up straighter in his chair and looked from side to side. "What's the bunkhouse?"

"A cabin on my property," said Jax. "I want you there within the hour. Help Red supervise the upgrades."

"Uh…" Logan shifted uncomfortably in his chair.

"I'm sort of having a party tonight. I mean, I know this is more important, and if you need me there I'll go, but—"

"A party?" snapped Jax.

Logan cleared his throat. "Yes sir. You said you'd be there, actually. Sort of a housewarming party for my new condo."

Jax furrowed his brow. "I don't give a rat's ass about—"

"Hawk can stay at the bunkhouse with me," interrupted Cowboy. "Once Red's got the security perimeter in place, we can all stop by the party for a bit."

Jax and Cowboy exchanged a look. "Fine," said Jax.

Logan smiled. "Glad you can make it, sir."

Jax showed his teeth. "Let's get started. We only have two or three hours before dark."

CHAPTER 29

I F JAX WAS the Tin Man, then this office was the inside of his big, empty chest.

The walls held pictures of Jax with five star generals and two US Presidents. There were two degrees, one from Harvard and one PhD she never knew he had, but it failed to give him personality or actual flesh and blood.

Jessa's eyes drifted over shelves of books about history and tactical decision-making, and it occurred to her that even with good decisions, history was still bound to repeat itself unless people learned, but that never seemed to happen.

That was why people like Jax and companies like HERO Force had something to do, lest they sit around here twiddling their thumbs.

She sat down at his desk with a sigh. She didn't

know what she was looking for, she only knew she had not found it. She started opening drawers, unconcerned with Jax's privacy. He'd gone through everything she owned. If he didn't want her going through his things, he shouldn't have left her in here alone.

The first thing that surprised her was the gun. In a place like this, everyone had a weapon all the time, but to find one in an unlocked drawer was alarming. She checked the chamber. It wasn't loaded, and she slipped it back inside the drawer and opened the next one.

Whiskey. Arguably, Jax's best friend.

No surprise there.

She pulled open the bottom drawer and her heart fell out of her chest. There, next to a few cigars, was a small framed picture of Ralph and Jax laughing.

Her chest tightened as she brought the picture close to her face. They were wearing fatigues, and she recognized it must have been taken in their navy days. From the obvious youth on their faces, it was likely shortly after they met and before Jessa was even in the picture.

Those two were always laughing together. Come to think of it, the only time she'd seen Jax really laugh was with Ralph. They were friends—good friends—and finding this little piece of her heart tucked away in Jax's desk drawer seemed like the only thing in the entire space that showed he was capable of feeling.

CHAPTER 30

J AX WALKED BACK to his office wondering what he
would find. He never knew how Jessa was going to
respond, never knew if she would be happy or sad,
angry or glad. It should have driven him crazy.
Instead, it just made her fascinating.

Nothing could have prepared him for what he
found. She was sitting at his desk, the framed picture of
Ralph and him in her hands, crying.

He stopped short, and she looked up to meet his
stare. "We both loved him, didn't we?" she asked.

Jax ground his back teeth together as he moved to
her and perched a hip on his desk. He could think of a
thousand things he'd rather talk about, but he only
said, "Yes."

She nodded. "I'd forgotten how you two used to
laugh together." She wiped at her cheek. "I think it

was easier if I forgot you were his friend."

"I haven't forgotten."

She put the picture down and leaned back in her chair. "What you said before, about us not doing anything wrong, I know you're right about that. I know my head is still screwed on backwards and six kinds of sideways." She shook her head. "That's why I was moving to Savannah. I had to get out of that house, away from the memories that live there. I was really trying to make a fresh start."

"Why did you come to the bar that night?"

He was afraid he already knew the answer to that question, but he still thought he had to ask it. Had she really come there with the intention of getting pregnant? Or had she been lonely, and he was the lucky man who just happened to be there?

She met his eyes, guilt shining in their depths. "I did it on purpose, Jax. Is that what you're asking me? Did I get pregnant on purpose? Because I did."

He shook his head. "No. When you decided to come to the bar, did you want to talk to me?"

She frowned. "I see, you're looking for a way to lessen the blame." She stood up. "I hate to disillusion you, but I went to the bar that night hoping to get pregnant." She crossed her arms, no longer meeting his eyes.

"By me?"

She nodded. "It made some twisted kind of sense. I

know that's not right, and I knew it wasn't right then, either. But everything that happened that night was exactly what I was hoping would happen."

"You were grieving."

"Dammit Jax, don't make excuses for me. I went to that bar to seduce you, in hopes I got pregnant, so I could be a mother. You were never part of the plan."

He lifted his chin. "Beyond the obvious, of course."

She flushed. "You weren't supposed to find out. You weren't supposed to get hurt."

"Isn't that what you wanted? To hurt me?"

"No."

He scoffed.

"I just wanted a baby, Jax. I didn't think beyond that. I knew it was wrong and I did it anyway. I was in such a dark place, and there you were, and I couldn't see past trying to get back what I'd lost." She put her hands on her hips and closed her eyes. "Forget it. I can't do this anymore. Are we done here? I'd really like to get out of this place."

Jax led the way through the labyrinth that was HERO Force, back out through reception, and down the elevator. He stole a sideways glance at her as they descended. She'd almost seemed sorry for what she'd done, though she'd stopped short of a real apology.

Because she's not sorry for the baby.

And what about him? Was he sorry for the life they'd created?

Not for a second.

They got to his truck and he opened her door for her, earning him a glare, and he couldn't help but smirk. He surprised himself by saying, "Logan is having a party tonight. I said we'd go."

"Seriously? What are you going to tell the guys?"

"I'll tell them the same thing I told Cowboy. The truth. You and I are having a baby together. And if anybody has a problem with that, that's just too goddamn bad."

CHAPTER 31

JESSA TWISTED AND turned in front of the mirror, pleased with what she saw. Once she figured out Jax was serious about going to this party, she pointed out she had nothing to wear. So they'd gone shopping, with Jax looking even more uncomfortable than normal—if that was possible—as he followed her around the women's department. To her surprise, many of the clothes that normally would have fit her were now too small around the middle. Her baby was growing quickly.

Their baby.

Theirs.

She shook her head. She was not going to think about that tonight.

She'd never met Logan, but the idea of a party held definite appeal. It seemed the last several months were some long, drawn-out high drama that desperately needed comic relief. Her eyes went to the bodice of her dress, the full globes of her breasts subtly on display.

I wonder if he'll like it.

She met her eyes in the mirror.

Was that what she wanted? For Jax to find her attractive? The picture of Ralph and Jax from Jax's desk drawer had softened her heart. Then Jax had been looking for ways to excuse her behavior and she'd gotten so choked up she'd barely been able to hide it from him.

There was a knock at the door. "Yes?"

"Are you about ready? Hawk and Cowboy have got the security system all set to go, so we can head out anytime." She pulled open the door, surprised to see him in a bright blue polo shirt that brought out his eyes and a pair of jeans that fit him like a bull rider in a cigarette ad.

She licked her lips.

Wow.

"You look nice," he said.

She smiled, more pleased than she should be that he'd noticed. "What is this, some sort of truce or something?"

He grinned a truly warm smile, sending shivers down her arms. "It's not a bad idea. Just for tonight. We can go back to hating each other tomorrow if you still want to." He winked.

She exhaled a breath it seemed she'd been holding for days. "That would be great."

They walked outside and got back in his car. "Tell me about Logan. I've never met him."

"Doc is okay. He's young, and greener than a grasshopper's wings. He's from the NSA, not the SEALs, and sometimes he just doesn't get it. He wouldn't be so bad if he wasn't so damn eager to please."

"How long has he been working for you?"

"About a year. Smart as all hell, but I keep getting the feeling I'm a high school guidance counselor instead of a black ops commander."

They pulled up in front of a small two-story building, and Cowboy and Hawk came bounding out to the truck.

"Who's ready to party?" yelled Cowboy.

Hawk raised both hands in the air. "I am!"

Jessa found herself smiling at the two men. Hawk came around to Jessa's window. "Hey, sweetheart, long time no see." He kissed her cheek before climbing into the back of the extended cab.

"Hi, Trevor. How've you been?"

"Good."

"Hawk's got himself a girlie friend," said Cowboy, now sitting behind Jax.

She turned around in her seat. "Is it serious?"

He looked so happy when he said, "Yeah. I think it is."

"Well, that's awesome," she said.

Jax pulled onto the road.

"I've got me a girlie friend, too," said Cowboy. "Sixteen cheerleaders from the community college and a cross-dresser named Moe."

Jessa laughed, and it felt so good. When was the last time she had laughed with friends?

By the time they arrived at the party, she was feeling more relaxed than she'd been in ages.

Jax walked her inside, his hand lightly touching her back, and turned to her. "I need to track down Red and go over a few things. I won't be long."

"Okay. Cowboy will keep me company."

Cowboy wrapped his arm around her shoulders. "Well, hello there, good-looking. My name's Leo Wilson." He was laughing, then he lifted his head and his arm tightened on her shoulders.

"What is it?" She turned her head to follow his gaze to a curvy blonde with a sparkly blue dress and a lot of makeup. Even still, the woman was beautiful. "Who is that?" she whispered.

"Charlotte." He nodded to the woman and held up a hand in acknowledgment.

"Let me guess. Someone you know biblically?"

"Nope." He steered her away in the opposite direction. "Logan's sister."

"Ah. I think there's a story there somewhere."

Cowboy looked back over his shoulder. "If I knew she was going to be here, I would have steered clear."

"You don't like her?"

He dropped his arm and looked at her like she was crazy. "I like her a lot."

"Oh." She nodded. "Oh! I get it. You're trying to stay away from her because she's Logan's sister."

"Exactly. But she doesn't make it easy on me."

Jessa accepted a ginger ale from the bartender and turned to watch Charlotte. "I don't think I've ever seen you choke up in front of a woman, Leo."

"Yeah, well, if I have to keep the Wilson charm under wraps, I don't know what to say."

"Tell me about her."

He took a swig of beer. "She's loud, and she curses like a sailor." He turned his back to Charlotte and faced Jessa completely. "You see her nails?"

"Yes."

"Always long, always red, always killing me."

Jessa giggled. "I wouldn't think she was your type."

"Oh, she's not. Not at all, and I can't freaking handle it."

Charlotte was laughing, her head thrown back and her long neck exposed, a piercing cackle carrying over the noise of the other guests.

"Wow," said Jessa. "She is something, all right."

"I know, right? Why the hell does she have to be

related to Logan?"

Jessa shook her head. "Sometimes life is cruel, Leo. She's coming over here."

"Really?"

"Mmm hmm."

Cowboy puffed out his chest and Jessa shot him a look.

"Hey, Cowboy," said Charlotte. "You planning on coming over to say hello to me?" She opened her arms and hugged him, passing Jessa as she did.

She smelled of perfume, something really expensive or really cheap, Jessa wasn't sure.

"Well, howdy, Charlotte. I didn't know you were going to be here tonight," said Cowboy.

"I came into town for the mud-wrestling tournament at the fairgrounds. I'm a finalist."

Jessa tried not to laugh while Cowboy's eyes nearly fell out of his head.

Charlotte punched him in the arm. "Jesus, Cowboy. I'm fucking kidding."

He pointed at her. "You got me."

She took a healthy sip of her pink wine and held out a hand to Jessa. "I'm Charlotte O'Malley."

"Jessa McConnell."

"You two seeing each other?" she asked.

"Oh, no," said Jessa. "We're just friends."

Charlotte turned and winked at Cowboy. "What do you say you and me go out sometime, Leo?"

Jessa couldn't help but smile, forming an instant affection for Charlotte and enjoying the plight of poor Cowboy.

Cowboy clucked his tongue as his eyes roamed over Charlotte's bedazzled body. "As much as I would like that, I don't think your brother approves."

She leaned in toward him and whispered in his ear loudly enough for Jessa to hear, "I don't give a fuck whether or not he approves."

"Unfortunately, sweetheart, I have to give a fuck." He finished his drink. "There's a code, Charlotte. It ain't up to me."

She stuck her bottom lip out. "You're a grown man. Of course it's up to you."

He shook his head, looking to Jessa for support, but she pretended not to notice. "Logan's like family to me, honey. He's got my back when I'm out there wrestling the bad guys, and it wouldn't be right for me to go after his sister."

"Then maybe I'll just have to go after you." Charlotte turned back to Jessa. "It was nice to meet you, doll face." She began to walk away. "You'd better watch your back, Leo," she called over her shoulder. "I don't give up so easy."

Cowboy sighed heavily. "What the fuck am I going to do?"

Jessa laughed. "I don't know, but I hope I'm around to find out."

Cowboy was the life of the party, and soon he was pulled away by two very eager young women. So when Logan struck up a conversation, Jessa was relieved to have someone to talk to.

It turned out they had a lot in common, from their taste in music and movies to a love for travel and a similar quirky sense of humor. Logan talked about Jax and HERO Force as if they were the end-all be-all of American justice, and she smirked at his naïveté and desire to please his boss.

Good luck with that. He isn't an easy one to please.

Not that she'd ever tried, but she suspected it was a fruitless endeavor.

By the time Logan asked her out, she realized she should've seen it coming from the very beginning. She stammered, "Actually I am… not exactly…"

"Are you seeing someone?"

"Sort of. It's complicated… You seem really nice, and under different circumstances I'd say yes, but right now I don't think I really can."

Logan grinned, and the phrase boyish good looks popped into her mind unbidden. "You don't have to make up excuses," he said. "If you don't want to go out with me, just say so."

"No! It's not that, really. I would like to go out with you. It's just…"

Jax's voice behind her made her jump. "It's just that she's having my baby."

She watched in horror as Logan's face went from charming to terrified in the space of a single breath. She was blushing furiously now, more than a little upset at Jax's bold statement. "I'm sorry," she said.

Logan held up his hands. "No, I'm sorry. I didn't understand the two of you were a couple."

Jax put his arm around Jessa, and she squirmed beneath it. "We're not exactly a couple," she said.

Jax laughed. "You can't be much more of a couple than that, honey."

Logan made his excuses and walked away, leaving Jessa furious and embarrassed in his wake. She shook off Jax's arm. "What did you do that for?"

"I told you we would tell everyone the truth. Don't act surprised now."

"There's a nicer way to do this, you know. You don't have to be a complete asshole and make everyone uncomfortable."

Jax narrowed his eyes. "Is that what I was doing?"

"Yes."

"That's funny, because I thought I was keeping you from making a date with that young man," he ground out between clenched teeth.

She was taken aback by what appeared to be jealousy.

As if he even wanted her.

"So what if I was?" She looked from his head to his toes and back to his face again. "You and I are not an item. I'm free to date anyone I want to."

He grabbed her wrist. "You are carrying my child."

"So what?" She pulled her wrist out of his grip. "That doesn't mean I belong to you. It's bad enough I'll have to share this baby with you, but I sure as hell don't have to share myself."

"That's right, I'd forgotten. You only spread your legs because you were trying to ruin my life, not because you like me." He put his drink down. "We're leaving now."

She looked at his nearly empty cup. "How many of those did you have?"

"What difference does it make?"

She shrugged. "Just wondering if I have to drive your drunk, obnoxious ass home or if you can do it yourself."

"It's unsweetened iced tea, Jessa. I'm obnoxious sober, too." He grabbed her by the elbow and turned her around. "Now say good night to everyone so we can get the hell out of here."

CHAPTER 32

J AX DROVE HOME in silence, tormented by his own thoughts. There was no denying he'd been jealous of Logan from the moment he saw them talking across the room, Logan's body language screaming he was interested in Jessa. Jealous because the only man he wanted looking at her that way was himself.

So much for believing I hate her.

He was angry, for sure, but that was a very different thing than hating her. He should have realized the interest he had in her since the moment they first met years before would not be so easily shaken. Yes, she'd betrayed him by intending to take away his child, and that should have put him off her scent forever, but damn it all to hell, he still wanted her.

Maybe that's not such a bad thing.

If he could find a way to put that behind him,

maybe even forgive her, it might still be possible for them to share this child.

He changed lanes, surreptitiously glancing in her direction. Her posture clearly said *still angry, and not likely to get over it anytime soon.* Hell, he was angry, too. The question was, could they find a way to feel something besides anger?

Jax thought back to another car ride, the eighteen hours he'd driven to first tell her they'd killed Steele. He'd spent several of those hours facing the fact that he was interested in Jessa for himself. Apologizing to his dead friend.

Now Jessa was pregnant with his baby, and he had even more reason to pursue her.

Not less.

She lied to you. She's no better than Linda.

But Linda hadn't been carrying his child.

She'd made sure of that.

Keep your friends close and your enemies closer.

He could pursue Jessa, have a relationship with her, maybe even raise the baby as a family. But he would never give her his heart, never trust her after what she had done. It was the only way to move forward from here.

CHAPTER 33

J ESSA WALKED INTO Jax's house and threw her
purse on the counter with no intention of slowing
down on her way to the guest room. She thought of
her restraints from the night before and knew she could
not suffer the same humiliation tonight.

She rounded on him. "If you try to tie me down to
that bed again, I will kick your ass, so help me God. If
you want me to stay here, you'd better find another
way, because you know if it's up to me, I will head out
that door and never look back."

He crossed his arms and widened his stance. "Yes,
you've made that quite clear."

The smug look on his face and his calm, cool de-
meanor caused her temper to explode. She pointed at
his chest. "You had no right to tell Logan to back off. I
am not your property, and I can do with my body and

my life whatever I want."

"Is that what you want, Jessa? Do you want to go out with Logan?"

"No! I want you to understand that I am not yours."

"You've made that quite clear tonight, too." His chest and bulging biceps were right at her eye level like a brick wall she would never be able to get through.

"But there's one thing I don't think you understand." He let his head drop forward, his eyes connecting with hers like a magnet to ferrous metal. "You have no idea what it was like," he said, his voice deep and throaty, "when I was watching you with him tonight. I wanted to throttle him."

Jessa shook her head. "Oh, please."

He uncrossed his arms, lightly taking her by the shoulders, and the air became charged with electricity.

"You were laughing, and he was looking at you like he wanted to see you naked, and I knew every thought in his head. I wanted to punch him in the jaw and carry you out of there over my shoulder."

Jessa dropped her eyes to his chest.

He reached up and gently touched her cheek, lifting her face to his. "I didn't want him looking at you like that. I didn't want him looking at you at all."

"He wasn't doing anything wrong."

"No, he wasn't. Not like I want to do." With that, he lowered his mouth to hers and kissed her, a gentle, seductive kiss that promised so much more if she was willing.

"We were supposed to have a truce," she said.

"I know."

"I was looking forward to it."

He pushed his nose lightly against hers, putting her mouth in position for his kiss once again. "We can have the truce now."

He nipped at her lips with his own, teasing her, and she wanted him to kiss her for real. How could she want that? Did she have no self-respect?

"This doesn't feel like a truce," she said. "This feels like you're winning."

"Let me make love to you tonight, and I promise you we'll both win."

His words had her melting inside, but she was scared. The first time they had sex, she expected to find it unpleasant and had been shocked when her body responded to his with such force. She hadn't wanted to feel that way, had simply wanted him to take his pleasure and leave her be.

Now she wanted the whole package. Because if she was going to sleep with Jax again, she had to accept it would be pleasurable.

Immensely pleasurable.

The stress of the last few days was catching up to her. Images of Ralph floated through her mind, she and Ralph together, Ralph and Jax tucked into a drawer in Jax's office. Could she simply let him be forgotten? Could she move on to his best friend and let go of the guilt that threatened to drown her?

I want it so badly.

She thought about what it would mean. Making love to Jax. Letting herself touch and be touched. Deliberately making him feel good, letting him overpower her if he wished. She took a deep breath in and held it, her eyes searching his. Would he be patient with her? Would he let her find her own physical release as she was able, or would he force his hand, making her feel exposed and vulnerable as she had in the hotel?

You felt those things because you didn't want to enjoy being with him. Are you ready to let him touch you, let him stroke your sensitive places, and trust him with your response?

Her heart beat rapidly with anticipation.

Oh, yes.

She was ready. She'd gone too long without the joy of sex, the electric and spiritual connection to another human being, the animalistic dedication to touch and physical release. She knew this man was capable of making her body sing, and she craved him like the cracked earth craves water.

"I'm scared," she said.

"I know." He lightly ran his fingers through her hair. "But you don't have to be."

The sensation of his short nails against her scalp

made her purr, and she let her eyes close, then reached out and touched his chest. He was warm and solid beneath her hands, the beating of his heart palpable through his skin, the air heavy with the scent that was uniquely his.

He was flesh and blood, stimulus and response. He was alive, and she longed to hold him inside her. Her fingers curled into the fabric of his shirt and pulled him toward her, lifting her head and kissing him full on the mouth.

He tasted like tea, and it struck her that the last time they'd had sex, he'd been drunk. Would he be the same kind of lover he had been then? Or would he be more mechanical, less sensual?

The idea gave her pause, but no sooner had she thought it than he took control of the kiss, dipping his tongue into her mouth and teasing her just as she remembered.

His arms were around her waist, and his hands came up to stroke her back, the sensation quieting the questioning voice in her head. She felt warm desire unfurling inside of her. She wanted to enjoy every touch, every experience she was given before moving on to the next one, like savoring a box of chocolates.

She dropped her head to his shoulder, inhaling the scent of him before trailing kisses from his collarbone to his ear. He moaned, the deep tenor of his voice vibrating the muscular column of his neck beneath her mouth.

He grabbed the back of her head and brought her face to his. She felt completely exposed, totally at his mercy.

"I want you in my bed," he said, taking her hand and pulling her behind him. They passed the guest room with her bindings atop the sheets, and she looked forward to giving them a try another time. Right now she wanted to lie between the covers that smelled of him, her bottom in the curve of the mattress where he slept night after night, wanted to see what that space was like.

At the end of the long hallway, he pushed open the door into a room full of windows, the blue glow of moonlight streaming through their panes. In the center of the room was a wide, tall bed with thick posts of twisting wood. She walked to a bedpost, her hand running along the carved spiral, and Jax came up behind her, pulling back her hair and kissing her neck. She arched her back, looking for him, and he fitted himself against her bottom.

She could smell the earthy spice of cinnamon mixed with soap, cologne, and the essence of him on the air. Jax lifted her shirt and she raised her arms, allowing him to pull it over her head. Then he eased her bra straps down to her elbows, leaving a trail of sensation across her shoulders and arms.

She wanted more of him, wanted his hot skin beneath her hands and her breasts against the solid wall of his chest. She spun around.

"Oh, yes," murmured Jax, taking her breasts in his hands and teasing her nipples to attention.

She was tugging at his shirt, pulling it out of his pants and over his head with hasty fingers, desperate to feel skin on skin. She pushed the sides of his shirt back over his shoulders and down to his forearms, the fabric temporarily keeping him restrained.

She looked her fill at his impressive chest, sculpted muscle rolling over bone. Then she moved lower, lightly caressing him and taking his nipple into her mouth before loosening the buckle at his waist. She freed him of his belt and unzipped his fly, nuzzling his hard cock with her face and lips through the fabric of his briefs.

Jax swore under his breath and hauled her up, pushing her backwards onto the bed and climbing on top of her. She spread her legs, welcoming him between them as her breathing got heavier with need. He felt so good pressing her down, the weight of him alone enough to make her weep with joy, and she writhed against him, desperate for more.

He removed her bra and the newly developed fullness of her breasts made them fall to the side, heavy and tender.

He spoke just inches from her ear, his voice husky and rough. "I love the changes in your body. That I did this to you."

She loved sharing herself with him, her body and every bit of what was taking place inside her. It was as if by allowing herself to be with this man, she was letting him into her pregnancy, into her life, and there was no going back.

He took one breast in his hand and measured its fullness with his palm, lightly squeezing her before taking her tip in his mouth and tasting her with his tongue. She bucked wildly beneath him. He opened wide and took more of her in his mouth, and she called out and pulled his head tightly against her.

"You're so sensitive," he said. His hand slipped between her legs and pressed against her swollen mound. "Are you sensitive here, too?"

She made a funny noise as she pressed back against his hand. "Yes." The sound of her voice was breathy and desperate to her ears.

Then he was taking off her pants and pulling at her panties. She opened her legs for him again and he settled on top of her, naked. The feel of his erection pressed against her pushed her over the top. She wanted him inside of her, wanted to see if it was as good as she remembered, and she pressed her head back against the pillow.

Then he was kissing her, deep, desperate kisses, and she kissed him back with the urgency that was building between her legs. His cock was poised at her entrance, and she thought she might die if he didn't get inside of her.

"Now, Jax. I need you."

"Open your eyes."

She forced her heavy lids apart, Jax's intense gaze fastening itself to her stare.

He eased inside of her, his girth forcing her wide open, and she called out in pleasure from the sensation. She'd forgotten what sex was like during pregnancy, the heightened sensitivity and the puffy feel of her womanly walls around him.

Ralph had loved it.

"Do you feel how swollen I am?" she asked Jax. "How tight?"

"God, yes."

"It's because of the baby. Your baby growing deep inside of me, Jax."

He groaned loudly, thrust into her deeper, harder. "God, you feel so good. Am I hurting you?"

"No." She dug her nails into his back. "I want more."

His deep, torturous thrusts forced her body to accommodate his size and set off an avalanche of feeling inside her. She screamed softly. He reached under her arms and held her shoulders in his hands, holding her still while he thrust himself hard and fast into her body.

Her orgasm exploded like a thousand scattering pieces, then Jax was coming, too, his cock buried to the hilt inside her, emptying his seed at the entrance to her womb once more.

CHAPTER 34

JESSA LAY IN the darkness, listening to Jax's even breathing and stroking his head. Tonight had been everything she had hoped for, and everything she feared. She could feel herself warming to this man and knew she would be unable to confine the feeling to the bedroom.

Would that be so bad?

She closed her eyes. It felt good to be loved. Physically and emotionally.

Is that what you think this is?

She was such a fool.

Jax didn't love her. He had never even pretended to care for her. If anything, his feelings for her leaned more toward hatred and contempt, and she didn't blame him for that. She'd done him a terrible disservice.

She frowned, examining her guilt, and she did feel guilty. Somehow over the past few days, she had come to know that tricking him as she did was wrong, no matter what she'd lost or who was ultimately responsible. Tears burned the backs of her eyes as she thought of her lost husband and child.

Jax hadn't wanted those things to happen. He had loved Ralph, too, and he would have protected them if he could have.

It had been Ralph's decision to go after Steele. The tears welled up in her eyes and spilled onto her cheeks, quickly disappearing into Jax's pillow. As much as she wanted to have someone to blame, she knew in her heart Jax had made the best decision he could with the information available to him.

Of course he had. He was a good leader, and he wouldn't have let his friendship with Ralph get in the way of a good tactical decision.

She was weeping openly now, holding on to Jax and praying he didn't wake up. She didn't know what she could possibly say to him to make him understand she was sorry for what she had done. Not sorry for the child but for her duplicity.

Jax stirred, and lifted his head. "What's wrong?"

She shook her head quickly.

"You're crying."

She cried harder, her quiet, shaking tears now loud, quaking sobs. "I shouldn't have done this. At the time, it seemed right, like the only thing that would serve up some kind of justice." She shook her head. "But it was wrong, and I'm so sorry for what that's done to you."

"Are we talking about tonight?" he asked.

She laughed through her tears. "No. Tonight was great. The first time." She met his eyes. "At the hotel. I was so lonely, Jax. I was so lonely, for so long. And then, there you were, and I blamed you, and I let myself forget you are human. That you had feelings, that you loved him, too." She rested her forehead against his. "It was so much easier to tell myself it was all your fault. I needed a villain, and you became my scapegoat."

He touched her cheek. "I understand."

"Then you brought me here, and I could see you weren't a villain at all, which meant I'd done something terribly wrong."

"It's okay."

"No, it's not okay. You're going to be a father. Your life will be different forever because of what I did."

"My life will be better."

She looked up, not believing what she'd heard. "What?"

"I'm starving. Do you want some ice cream?" He grinned and rolled out of bed, looking for his clothes.

She sat up, pulling the blankets up to cover herself

as she stared at his naked body. "How will your life be better, Jax?"

"I always wanted kids."

"But like this?" She swallowed. "With me?"

He pulled on his briefs and jeans, his face unreadable. "It isn't how I thought things would work out, if that's what you mean." He pulled on his shirt. "But I like you. I always have. Come on. I have chocolate and vanilla. There might even be some whipped cream."

What about you and me, Jax?

Her mind was screaming the question, but she didn't ask it. Instead, she narrowed her eyes and said, "Do you have any chocolate syrup?"

He smiled, and the transformation of his face was mesmerizing. "A woman after my own heart," he said.

At that exact moment, the bedroom window shattered into hundreds of pieces. Jessa heard herself screaming, but Jax was already in action, pulling her to a stand and quickly out of the room. Then it was dark, and he said, "Sixteen steps. Ready?" And she was being led down a blackened staircase, counting the steps as she went, to a musty room beneath the main floor.

A basement?

He was talking to someone as he pulled her through the space. "Someone fired at the bedroom window. Jessa is unhurt. I'm putting her in the safe room now. You two come in through the back of the house."

There was the screeching sound of metal on metal, then a light came on inside a small room with a couch, table, and four chairs. He grabbed a blanket and thrust it at her, reminding her she was naked, and she pulled it around her shoulders.

"Stay here," he said, placing the book she inherited on the table. She hadn't even noticed he grabbed it. "Lock the door when I leave. This is a safe room. No one will be able to get in unless you let them in."

"What about you?" she asked, surprised to hear her voice trembling.

"I have to help the others. There are clothes in the closet." He walked to a corner and unlocked a gun cabinet, but it was the back of his shirt that got her attention.

"Jax, you're bleeding!"

"I'm fine."

"But there's so much blood..."

He turned around. "Remember to lock it. Don't let anyone in."

She nodded her head vigorously, then watched in horror as he disappeared back into the blackness, and she locked herself inside the safe room with trembling hands.

CHAPTER 35

J AX WAS WISHING he had his night-vision monocular as he made his way up the steps and out of the basement.

Hawk's voice sounded in his ear. "One tango, thirty yards outside the front door and approaching fast. I'm a hundred yards behind him. He has a semiautomatic and plenty of ammo. I can reach him from here, but it won't be a kill shot."

"Negative," snapped Cowboy. "I have a good line of sight to the front door from inside the house. I'll take him out."

Whoever was after Jessa needed to be stopped once and for all, and Jax knew damn well there were probably more tangos out there just waiting to come in after this one.

He reached the top of the basement stairs and

hunkered down, crawling on his hands and knees. If their attacker was coming in the front door, he'd have plenty of time to cover Cowboy's six.

He felt light-headed and knew his injury was more severe than he first suspected. He was losing blood quickly, which meant it was just a matter of time before he lost consciousness.

Thank God Jessa was in the safe room. Jax's vision went dim, then returned again. He put his finger on the trigger of his weapon, hoping he could stay conscious long enough to kill the bastard.

He had to kill him for Jessa.

His mind was full of her, their night together, and the baby. A flash of Jessa as a mother, nursing their infant at her breast. His eyes closed and his head dipped, then he snapped it back up and opened his eyes, forcing his arms to hold up his weapon.

It was heavier than he could fathom.

"Cancel that!" yelled Hawk in his ear. "Tango is headed for the bedroom window. Copy that? Not for the front door, the same bedroom window he shot out. And we have another tango thirty yards out."

Jax's brain struggled to make sense of the words. His vision was now completely out of focus, and he couldn't bring it back. He looked up just in time to see a figure jump through the window over his head, but the swift movement made everything go black. He heard the sound of the other man's steps on the breaking glass and wondered how much time had passed.

He fought to open his eyes and failed. He had to stay awake, had to get Jessa out of danger once and for all. This time his eyes opened, the shadow of a man standing over him. Jax took the shot. A bright flash from the muzzle of the tango's gun was the last thing Jax saw before losing consciousness.

CHAPTER 36

*D*EAR GOD, THIS *book is boring.*

Jessa laid *The Manor* open, facedown on her lap, and looked at Jax. He was sleeping as he had been for the last several hours since his surgery. He'd lost a lot of blood, but they'd managed to save his injured kidney.

He was going to be okay.

When Cowboy came and got her from the safe room, she instantly knew something was wrong. Jax should've been there. He wouldn't have sent anyone in his stead unless he wasn't able to come himself.

"Let me in, Jessa."

"Where's Jax?"

"He can't come down here right now, sweetie. Open the door."

She unlatched the lock and pulled open the heavy

metal door. One look at Cowboy's face, and she'd started to scream. "No! This isn't happening again. This is not happening again!"

He had grabbed her upper arms. "Listen to me, Jessa. He's hurt. Shot. The ambulance is on its way, but you're a nurse. He needs your help."

She ran behind Cowboy up the stairs, the acrid smell of gunpowder polluting the air. "What happened to the other guy?"

"One tango down. That's the good news. But another one got away somewhere on the mountain."

They rounded the corner to the bedroom, and Jessa was struck by how much had changed since the last time she walked down this hallway.

He's going to be okay.

But even as she told herself that, she was back in her little yellow house and her happy little life as a wife and soon-to-be mother, her mouth open wide in horror as Jax told her Ralph had been killed. Her tongue had tasted like metal and blood rushed in her ears. The two moments melded together in her mind.

They entered the bedroom, Jax on the floor in a pool of his own blood.

Too much blood for anyone to survive.

She moved to kneel beside him, and Cowboy held out his hand to stop her. "Watch yourself, there's glass." He grabbed a pillow off the bed and handed it to her. She put it on the ground and kneeled on it.

Jax's face was so pale, so unlike his normal complexion. She put her hand on his neck and felt for a pulse. Forty.

His pulse was fucking forty.

The sound of a siren in the distance made the moment more surreal, as if the ambulance would never actually get here but would always be too far away. Too late to save Ralph. Too late to save Jax. She took his arm and pulled him onto his side, lifting his shirt in the back. Blood oozed from his wound.

"I need a clean towel or shirt, something."

Cowboy handed her a towel, which she pressed to Jax's back. "Press this here, firmly. Keep the blood from coming out," she said. She stood on shaking legs and ran to get a blanket to cover him with.

Jax was on the floor bleeding to death. Jax was standing in front of her, telling her Ralph was dead. If Jax was dead, then she was dead. The baby…

An alarm went off on the monitor next to the bed, snapping her attention back to the present. What the hell was the matter with her? Was that a panic attack?

She reached for Jax's hand and stared at his too-still face while a nurse came in and replaced his IV. His color was better, but that wasn't saying much.

"Matteo and Trevor were here earlier," she said, letting her fingers trace the lines on Jax's knuckles. "You were still in surgery. Trevor and Olivia are engaged. Did you know that already? She seems nice. I never thought I'd see him so taken with a woman. Figures she's a movie star." She let go of his hand and stood up. "That lawyer from Boston stopped by while they were here. Fred Bach. He said he needed to speak to you and would be back in an hour or so to see if you were awake."

Her eyes fell on the metal railing along the side of the bed, and she wished she could lie down beside him. She longed to put her arms around his body, to wrap him up with healing energy and be as close to him as she possibly could. But it wasn't just the hospital rules that kept her from doing so.

If he awoke, would he be happy she was here? Had she read too much into the few things he said at the end of their night together?

My life will be better.

Did he mean that? And was he happy only about the baby, or about her as well?

"I hope you meant me, too," she whispered.

But did she?

Did she really?

Already she'd almost lost him. She knew she couldn't handle being half of a HERO Force couple again, always wondering if he was okay, always praying for his safe return, being gone more than he was ever with her.

She needed stability, normalcy, both for herself and the baby.

No matter what happens, this child will always have a HERO Force member for a father.

She wouldn't be able to protect her baby from that fate. Her hand went to her abdomen, lightly stroking her growing belly. Cowboy's words ran through her mind. *Your kid couldn't do better.* But what good was the world's greatest father if he was never around, or managed to get himself killed protecting other people?

She sighed and sat back in her chair. She picked the book up off the table, forcing herself to read. She couldn't even finish one page.

"I hate this book. The story is stupid, and I can't figure out why anybody would pay money for this thing. I mean, who wants to read a book about an old rich family with no problems, anyway?" She moved to fold the book back over and, in the process, fanned the pages ever so slightly.

A picture appeared, a tiny and perfectly detailed little painting she recognized immediately. It was the mansion overlooking the ocean she had seen in the conference room of the lawyer's office in Boston. Her mind whirled, working to fit the pieces of the puzzle together, knowing the answer was just a single turn of a piece away.

This book was intrinsically tied to the law firm.

She turned the volume around in her hands, seeing it in a new light. "This isn't a stupid book with no plot. It's a history of the Bach family."

As in Layton, Felder, Bach & Moore.

"Oh my God," she whispered, now frantically flipping through pages, knowing exactly what she was looking for—an obscure reference to the newborn child of the family housekeeper, Señora Cortez. She found it on page eighty-nine.

"The babe wasn't as round as Cortez's other children but paler in flesh and longer in limb. Reggie Moore noted no difference and went on to law school in the spring."

She closed the book and squeezed it against her chest. "I know who's trying to kill me."

Her eyes flew to the clock on the wall. The lawyer would be back any minute. Taking one last look at Jax, she prayed he would stay asleep and quickly ran from the room.

CHAPTER 37

J ESSA WALKED BRISKLY through the hospital cafeteria, her eyes scanning for Cowboy or Logan. Neither one of them was here.

Dammit. What was she going to do now?

She pulled out her cell phone, wishing she still had the numbers for the HERO Force guys in her contacts. Fortunately, she still remembered the number for headquarters.

"I need to speak to Leo Wilson please. It's an emergency."

"Who's calling?"

"This is Jessa McConnell. Ralph McConnell's widow."

"I'm very sorry, Ms. McConnell, but you are not on the priority call list. I'm afraid I can't put you through."

Frustration and fear had Jessa clenching her fists. "You listen to me. I'm at the hospital where Jax Andersson is recovering, I've got a seriously bad dude trying to kill me, one man I love has already died for you people, and I'm pregnant with the baby of another one. Now you better damn well put me through to Cowboy this instant!"

Silence hung on the line between them. "Hang on, transferring you now."

Jessa was nearly back to the elevator and pressed the button as she listened to Cowboy's phone ring in her ear.

"Leo Wilson."

"Cowboy! It's Jessa. Where are you guys?" The elevator doors opened and she got on with a small crowd of people.

"Logan here ain't never tried fajitas, so we stopped by Sexy Hombre's for a skillet."

That restaurant was at least a quarter mile away. "I need you back here now. I know who's after me. It's all in the book. I figured it out, but now I don't know what the hell to do. Jax is still out cold and the bad guy lawyer is due back here any minute." She was aware of the curious glances she was receiving from other people in the elevator and turned her back to them.

"Go to the lobby," said Cowboy. "Stay where there are a lot of people. We're on our way."

"Hurry, Leo. Please." She disconnected the call

and turned back around. Her eye caught that of Fred Bach standing in the very back of the elevator, and her heart leapt in her chest. He was staring at her like a predator stared at its prey, and she knew he'd heard every word.

The elevator doors opened and two construction workers got on, further crowding the already packed space. Jax's room was on the top floor of the hospital. If she did nothing, the crowd would thin until the only people remaining in the car were her and the lawyer, the man who wanted her dead.

Just as the doors were closing, she dashed between them and out of the car. From the corner of her eye she could see the lawyer making a move, heard him say, "Excuse me," but it was too late. The elevator doors closed behind her and she looked around at what was clearly a construction zone.

She began a desperate search for escape. There had to be a staircase, another way out of the building, but everything was covered in giant sheets of plastic, an eerie green glow the only light on the floor.

She pushed at door after door looking for an exit. "Is anyone here? Please, somebody help me!"

The sound of plastic rustling in the distance stopped her cold. The hair on the back of her neck went up. She wasn't alone. She couldn't head back to the elevator—that's where the noise came from. She could only go forward like a rat nearing the end of a maze.

A voice called out behind her. "I'm not going to hurt you, Maria. I just want the book. That's all."

Jessa was aware of the tap of her tennis shoes on the floor. She slipped them off and continued on in her socks. Even her breath was too loud. She pushed at this door and that, nearing the end of the hallway.

The very last door had two strips of yellow hazard tape across it, and it opened wide as she pushed it. Even though she was being careful, she nearly fell into the stairwell shaft. But the stairs were chipped out, their concrete and most of the steel supports missing, with only a few bars to hold the structure in place.

"The book has no value to you, Maria. It is only important to me. We can make a deal."

Jessa squeezed her eyes closed, swallowed against the knot in her throat. "What are you offering?" she asked. She was aware as she said the words they might be the last to escape her. If he had a gun, she would surely die here today. She reached up and pulled the hazard tape off the door.

Bach rounded the corner at the end of the hallway with a shuffle of plastic sheeting. They faced each other.

"Ten thousand dollars," he said. "An amount like that can change your life." He walked toward her, the click of his shoes ticking off the seconds until he reached her.

"I think one eighth of your law firm is worth a hell of a lot more than that. Don't you?"

He smiled affably. "What are you talking about?"

"It's all right here." She held up the book. "Señora Cortez's child was the son of Reggie Moore. Your grandfather, I assume?"

He didn't answer.

"Mine, too, it would seem."

"It's a simple story. It holds no legal weight." He took a step toward her. "Peter Hopewell can attest to its fiction."

"Peter Hopewell?"

"The heir of Harold Hopewell's estate."

She backed up, close now to the empty stairwell. "What did that cost you, Bach? Did you even consider that a simple DNA test will show you and I are cousins?"

In three quick steps, he closed the distance between them. "Not if you're not around to take it."

Before she knew what he was about, his hands were around her neck, squeezing. She dropped the book. Hours of self-defense lessons with her husband came back to her in an instant. Clasping her hands together, she pushed them high through the circle made by her attacker's arms, forcing his hands from her neck.

He grabbed her around her middle and kneed her in the belly, vicious pain robbing her of her breath before he hit her on the back of her neck, taking her down. Her mind screamed for her baby, begging her to protect her little one at all costs.

She rolled up like a pill bug, hugging her knees to her chest, and he kicked her in the back. Her defensive position didn't allow her to fight back. All she could think about was the stairwell.

She inched toward it.

"Where the hell do you think you're going?"

"Let me go. I won't tell anyone about the book."

He laughed. "Too late for that now." He kicked her again. "Get up."

If he was going to kill her, she had no reason to comply.

Protect your baby.

Keep this child safe.

She inched closer to the door. The book was only a foot away, and she reached for it.

He stepped on her hand and she cried out.

"Reading time is over," he said.

"You can't stand to see it in print, can you? Reggie Moore's illegitimate child screwing you over to this day."

He took his foot off her hand and squatted down beside her. "Not for long, Cortez. Your family should've stayed in the kitchen where they belonged." He stood back up, and she once again reached for the book. He kicked it away.

Jessa stared at it. It was mere inches from the door

to the empty stairwell. She got up on her hands and knees and crawled toward it.

"You don't listen very well, do you?" He kicked her in her ribs, an audible crack making her wince as she gasped in pain.

She had no weapons. No way to defend herself.

Nothing except the empty stairwell.

She continued to crawl. When she was four feet away, he began to laugh.

She crawled, the pain of her broken rib stabbing her in the side with every movement of her torso.

He stepped in front of her and bent down to pick up the book. She lunged for him, forcing her body upright and driving him into the doorway like a football player.

He fell sideways and cursed, working to get his balance before he realized what she had done. His scream echoed in the stairwell until he landed with a disturbing crack.

Jessa fell back to the ground, curling back into her ball, nothing but pain surrounding her, and waited for Cowboy and Logan to discover her location.

CHAPTER 38

J AX STOOD IN the hallway of the maternity ward, his eyes fixed on Jessa through the open doorway to her hospital room. He should've been there, dammit. He'd put her in harm's way without even realizing it. She might even have died.

"I'm very sorry, Mr. Andersson," said the doctor, some young medical student who'd done his best to explain placental abruption. In the end, all that mattered was they were losing the baby.

Cowboy thanked the doctor for the information, but Jax didn't have any words.

He walked into her room and sat down beside the bed. The machine was beeping and he stared at it, not comprehending for a moment. Two heartbeats. Hers and the baby's.

Jesus.

Were they just supposed to sit here and listen to it die?

Jessa opened her eyes and reached for his hand. He held it in his own, his thumb gently rubbing her skin. "What did the doctor say?" she asked.

"He said you need to get your sleep."

"The baby, Jax. How is the baby doing?"

His eyes locked with hers, the horrible truth needing no words to be conveyed.

"He's wrong, Jax! I can feel the baby kicking. Our baby is alive."

He nodded, tears falling onto his cheeks as he moved his head. "Yes. But the placenta is coming off the uterine wall. He said there's a chance it might stop, but in all likelihood—"

"I'm going to lose the baby." Her eyes glistened, but she did not cry. She moved over. "Come and lie next to me. Just be careful of my ribs." She lifted the covers for him to climb in beside her, and Jax knew he had never experienced such great happiness or sorrow.

She settled her head in the crook of his arm and placed his hand on her stomach beneath her hospital gown.

His tears were coming freely now, rolling down his cheeks and into her hair. He kissed her forehead. A tiny movement beneath his hand made him jump.

"You felt that?" she asked.

"Yes."

"She's a fighter, our daughter. Don't count her out just yet."

Their daughter. Their little girl. It was too much to image she might die, and he felt a renewed sympathy for losses Jessa had already sustained.

Please, God, let us keep this baby.

Jax fell asleep in Jessa's bed, listening to the monitor beat in time to their daughter's heart and wondering if he'd ever have the chance to hold her in his arms.

CHAPTER 39

J AX STOOD AT the window of Jessa's darkened hospital room, staring at the lights of the city below, a stray tear falling down his cheek. The irony of the moment wasn't lost on him, the slowing of his daughter's heartbeat at the very moment he realized two very important things.

He would be a good father, capable of showing emotion, and he loved his child's mother with all his heart.

He didn't deserve either one of them, but for this moment in time, they were here. He turned around and stared at Jessa sleeping in the bed, her pregnancy hidden by the bedcovers. But there was a baby inside her—he'd felt her kick—and it was a child they had made together. For his part, that baby came from love.

Moving to the chair beside her bed, he sat down

and rested his head on the cold metal bed rail. "I love you, Jessa," he whispered, knowing it had always been true and not even her deception could take that away.

"And I love you, baby."

The monitor that was beeping over his head beat quickly twice. Jax's head shot up and he stared at the screen, the little double heartbeat now a scratch on the screen. And in that silly moment that didn't mean anything, Jax knew deep in his heart that their baby would be okay.

The tears that had been dribbling from his eyes welled up freely, spilling over as joy coursed through him. He reached for Jessa's hand, clenching it tightly. She'd never doubted, not for a moment.

"Everything's going to be okay," he said.

Thank you.

An image appeared in his mind. He was holding his tiny baby girl in his arms with Jessa by his side, resting her head on his shoulder.

He exhaled a shuddering breath. "Everything's going to be okay."

CHAPTER 40

J AX ROUNDED THE corner into Jessa's hospital room, a bouquet of bright flowers in his hand. She was standing at the window, fully dressed, her bag closed on the bed.

"Good morning. Are you two ready to go?"

She grinned at him and nodded, a hand pressed to her stomach. "More than ready."

She'd been in the hospital almost a week with doctors making sure the baby was stable before they allowed Jessa to get up and walk around.

Jax had been here the better part of every day.

Rooting for their baby to survive had brought them closer together. They played stupid games and watched Jeopardy on TV. Jax liked it, and he'd already made up his mind he didn't want any of it to end.

He handed her the flowers. "For you."

"Thank you." She sniffed the blossoms and smiled.

"I've been thinking, maybe you should move in with me," he blurted.

"What?"

"This week here with you. I've enjoyed it."

"I'm not sure that's enough of a reason to move in together."

"I can think of more."

"I like you, Jax." She looked at the floor then met his eyes. "A lot. But I barely survived my first experience with HERO Force. I can't go back to living like that. Waiting for you to come home and always fearing the worst."

"So expect the best, not the worst. I love what I do, and I'm good at it. HERO Force is making a difference in this world. A positive difference."

"Then do it, Jax. But don't expect me to keep the home fires burning, because I can't do it. Not again."

Jax stared at her long and hard. "Even if I love you?"

She raised her chin.

"Even if you've made me happier in weeks than I've been all my life?" he asked. "I meant what I said that first night you stayed in my bed. My life is better now—with you and the baby—than it's ever been before."

"HERO Force is a deal breaker for me, Jax. I'm sorry. I care about you so much, but I just can't do it."

"This isn't the kind of love you can keep at arm's length, Jessa." He wasn't used to expressing his feelings, wasn't used to putting something so personal into words. "It's the kind of love that swallows you up whole and will change everything in your life if you let it."

She took his hand. "Will you let it, Jax? Will you let it change your whole life?"

She was asking about HERO Force. If he would give it up for her. The thought made him crazy, but so did the idea of losing her. He didn't see how he could live without either one of them.

He brought her hand to his lips, kissing the back of it, aware of just how much he had to lose. "It's not an easy thing to do, what you're asking."

"I know."

He nodded, unable to tell her what she wanted to hear but equally unable to deny her request. "Don't give up on me yet, Jessa."

"I'm having your baby. I'm not going anywhere." She shrugged her shoulder. "Anymore, that is."

CHAPTER 41

SIX MONTHS LATER

COWBOY WALKED IN Jax's office. "What's up, chief?"

"We got a call from a liaison for the British monarchy. It seems Princess Violet is getting married to a member of the French National Assembly next week, and she's adamantly refusing to bring her security detail on the honeymoon. They've asked for someone from HERO Force to travel along on the same cruise, keeping an eye on the royal couple, preferably without their knowledge."

Cowboy furrowed his brow. "Maybe I'm behind on the tabloid gossip, but I've never even heard of Princess Violet."

"Daughter of Prince Bertram, sixth in line to the British throne."

"Ah. So, like the Beverly Hillbillies of the monarchy."

"That's exactly right." Jax laughed. "I figured you wouldn't mind a working cruise through the Caribbean."

Cowboy leaned back in his chair. "I think I might be able to squeeze it in my schedule."

Jax stood and grabbed his jacket. "Have Logan set you up with the reservation and whatever you'll need for surveillance and possible defense."

"Expecting any trouble?"

"Nope." He walked to the door. "I'm on my way to the doctor." He smiled widely. "Jessa's got another ultrasound today."

"You guys ever find out the sex?"

"No. Jessa's convinced it's a girl. I'd be happy either way." He took his keys from a hook on the wall. "Oh, and one more thing. The cruise is for couples only."

Cowboy grinned wickedly. "I think I might be able to find a lady to accompany me."

"Have Logan get somebody from the Academy. Just in case."

Cowboy nodded. "Will do."

"Leo, I've been thinking about bringing some women on full-time. Maybe another SEAL, too. Jessa's really digging in her heels about me spending so much time with HERO Force."

"Still won't marry you, huh?"

He shook his head. "Swears she'll never marry another guy from the team."

"Do you believe her?"

"I think if I cut back my hours, maybe promote a worthy member of the force and hire some new blood, she just might let me slide." He checked his phone. "I've gotta run."

Cowboy stood up. "I'm pretty worthy, you know."

Jax laughed. "Do a good job in the Caribbean. We'll talk when you get back."

CHAPTER 42

"**W**HAT THE HELL do you care if I go out with him or not?" asked Charlotte.

Logan held his head in his hands. "Do you have any idea what this job means to me? Cowboy is like my boss—"

"I thought Jax was your boss."

"Well, yes, technically. But Cowboy is more senior than me, and he's the unofficial leader of the team. If you go out with him, I'm fucked."

She frowned, her fuchsia lipstick accentuating the downward turn of her mouth. "What's that supposed to mean?"

"All of your relationships end badly."

"Of course they do, idiot. If they didn't end badly, they wouldn't end."

Logan took a laptop and several files out of his

briefcase. "Tell me you're messing with me, that you're just pretending you don't understand why this is a problem. Because if you're being sincere, I don't even know how to explain it to you."

She pulled out a chair and sat next to him at the table. "He likes me, Logan."

"So what? Lots of guys like you."

She shrugged. "Sure, lots of loser assholes like Rick. Not too many stand-up guys like Cowboy."

Logan sighed heavily. She was pulling out the Rick card, and he didn't appreciate it. Her ex-husband had done a real number on her. "I'm sorry, Charlotte. Why don't you go on a trip or something? You got all that money in the divorce settlement. So hop on a plane and go see the world. Experience new things. Maybe even meet a guy better than Cowboy."

She met his eyes. "You think so?"

"You want to know what I really think?" He put his hand over hers. "You're pretty damn special, sis, and one of these days you're gonna find a great guy who knows it."

"Thanks, Logan."

"You only live once, right?" His cell phone rang, and he took it into the other room. Charlotte looked at the papers spread out in front of Logan's computer. Cruise ship reservations for Cowboy to the Caribbean next week on a couples-only cruise. Her eyes went to the screen. There was the confirmation for Leo Wilson and Abigail Browning. Charlotte frowned.

What would she give to be on that cruise with him?

You only live once.

She shot a glance at the doorway, Logan still deep in conversation at the far end of the house. Before she could talk yourself out of it, she sat in front of his computer and scribbled down the cruise information. Logan had suggested she go on a vacation, hadn't he? Well, she was going to go on a vacation with an adventure built right in.

She left the room, a giggle on her lips and a new-found spring in her step. Charlotte O'Malley finally had something to look forward to.

CHAPTER 43

S YLVIA CORTEZ SPOKE in broken English, a little girl on either side of her on the worn sofa. "I don't understand."

Jessa rubbed her stomach, the size of which had easily doubled in the last three weeks alone. With just a month to go until her due date, she smiled at one of the girls and thought of her own daughter. "Is there someone who can translate for us?" she asked.

Sylvia spoke in Spanish to the taller of the two girls, who ran out the front door. Sylvia turned back to Jessa. "You like coffee? Decaf?"

"No, thank you. I'm fine." She picked up the book, gently fingering its pages. Logan had found Maria Elena's next of kin after an exhaustive search, and Jessa knew it was unlikely this family had ever met their distant cousin, but Maria Elena was about to give them a great gift nonetheless.

A tall, handsome boy came inside with the girl who'd gone in search of a translator. "Juan," said the girl.

Jessa stood and shook his hand. "My name is Jessa McConnell, and I've been looking for Sylvia for a long time." She handed the book to Sylvia with a smile. "She's been given a great inheritance from a distant cousin."

Jessa explained who Maria Elena was and what had happened to her. The boy's eyes went wide as he repeated what she'd said in Spanish.

"This book proves Maria Elena was entitled to a one-eighth share of a large law firm in Boston."

She nodded to the boy, who translated again.

"The lawyers would like to buy out your share for fourteen million dollars."

The boy gave a loud yelp and Jessa laughed. Sylvia leaned forward on the edge of the couch. Jessa watched Sylvia's face as the boy translated the good news.

The woman burst out screaming and the girls broke out in smiles. "Inheritance?" Sylvia asked, reaching for Jessa's hands.

"Yes. An inheritance just for you and your family."

Sylvia jumped up and down, laughing, pulling Jessa's hands with her. "Rich?"

Jessa laughed. "Yes, you're rich." She thought of the terrible things the inheritance had brought to her own life, but then again, she wasn't the rightful heir.

And it brought you Jax.

They'd been spending almost all of their time together. At first she'd insisted he not stay over more than twice a week, as if the boundary could keep her heart out of danger. But she was never able to push him out the door when all she wanted was to snuggle into his arms.

Now Jax was asking her to marry him, and as much as she didn't like him working for **HERO** Force and him traveling so much, she knew she'd be hard pressed to say no much longer.

She just had to find a way to deal with the fear.

She drove to the cemetery and sat on a bench beside Maria Elena's grave, telling the other woman about Sylvia and the family who would receive the money from the law firm settlement.

"Thank you for letting me use your name, Maria. You changed my life for the better."

Jax had told her something similar once, that his life was better with her in it, and she smiled at the memory. Her eyes went back to the gravestone. Maria Elena was born just one year before Jessa.

Life is short. Don't you want to live it to its fullest?

It was so hard to separate Jax from **HERO** Force in her mind, to peel apart the man and the danger he surrounded himself with every day.

"What if he gets hurt? What if he dies?"

I will be happy I loved him for as long as I could. Just like Ralph.

No one was guaranteed a long life. No one was guaranteed anything beyond this moment.

"And I want to share this moment with Jax," she said. She wiped a tear from her cheek. She wasn't going to waste another moment, not a single one. "Thanks, Maria."

Moving her awkward body as fast as she could, she made it back to her car and drove to **HERO** Force headquarters.

CHAPTER 44

J AX WAS READING over the draft of his new business plan for HERO Force. Cowboy would take over Jax's role, with Jax moving to a purely supervisory position.

Unless he really needed to blow something up.

"Jax?"

He lifted his head from the papers on his desk to find Jessa standing in the doorway. "Hey. What are you doing here?" He knew how much she hated this office, how much it reminded her of the past. "Everything okay?"

She nodded, closing the door behind her and walking toward him. "Everything's perfect. I gave Sylvia Cortez the good news."

"Oh, yeah? That must have been fun."

"It was. And then I stopped by to tell Maria it was

all taken care of. I think she was happy."

He grinned at her assignation of moods to the dearly departed. "I'm sure she was."

"But I realized, there's one more thing I have to do before I can move on with my life." She walked around his desk, perching her hip on the edge, and he stroked her leg from her ankle to her knee.

"What's that?"

"I have to tell you how much I love you."

He sucked in a breath and held it. He knew it. Of course he knew it, but to hear the words after so much time was like getting a gift he hadn't expected to receive.

She bit her lip, and her eyes shone brightly. "I've thought it a thousand times. I'm sorry it took me so long to say."

He stood up, hope swelling in his chest, and put his arms on her waist. "Does this mean you'll marry me?"

"Let me finish. I love you, and I accept that HERO Force is just as important to you as I am."

"No, it's not."

She kept talking. "You do incredible things here. Yes, they're dangerous, and yes, that drives me absolutely insane, but they're incredible nonetheless. I don't want you to stop."

"I said, it's not as important to me as you are, Jessa."

"It's not?"

"I'm cutting back my hours at HERO Force. Putting Cowboy in charge. He's earned it, and I want to make sure I see my daughter grow up. I want to be there for you." He'd already let his obsession with HERO Force destroy one marriage. He wouldn't make the same mistake again.

Her face lit up. "You're sure?"

"I'm positive. I love you, Jessa." He let his hand trace her face from her temple to her jaw, and kissed her. He was swamped with gratitude.

Her kisses were grew more passionate, and he smiled at his very pregnant, very horny, soon-to-be-wife.

She yanked her face away from his. "Uh oh." Her eyes were wide. "My water just broke."

Adrenaline shot into his bloodstream. "That's not supposed to happen yet. Are you sure?"

"Oh, I'm sure all right." She came to a stand, looking behind her. "Oh, God, I'm sorry about your desk."

"That's not my desk. That's Cowboy's desk. You ready to have a baby?"

"What if it's too early?"

"It's only twenty days, honey, I think she'll be fine."

"Right. You're right. It's only twenty days." She took a deep breath.

He'd never been happier in his whole life than he was in this moment. "Then let's go have a baby."

Charlotte didn't plan on this much trouble when she decided to crash Cowboy's cruise

BUY HARBORED BY THE SEAL

Sign up for Amy Gamet's mailing list

http://eepurl.com/yVjV1

or text BOOKS to 66866

ALSO BY AMY GAMET